PRAISE FOR NORTH AMERICAN LAKE MONSTERS

"My favorite collection from the last 5 years." — Sarah Langan

"A bleak and uncompromising examination of 21st century masculinity through lenses of dark fantasy, noir, and horror. Ballingrud is an important figure in North American letters." — Laird Barron

"What Nathan Ballingrud does in *North American Lake Monsters* is to reinvigorate the horror tradition." — John Langan, *Los Angeles Review of Books*

"Dark, quirky stories." — *Charlotte Observer*

"Ballingrud's lyrical and intense stories play on deeply personal fears and anxieties of the social outcast, the people who struggle to maintain relationships (spousal, parental, etc). People who are us. And like Daniel Woodrell and Donald Ray Pollack, Ballingrud's stories pack an authentic emotional punch. . . . Ballingrud's stories will keep you up at night, and you'll continue to obsess over them for many days after." — Paul Tremblay

"Ballingrud's debut collection uses complex characters and startlingly beautiful language to reinvent the horror genre. In Ballingrud's grim landscapes we encounter the supernatural as a chink in the human: sometimes terrifying, sometimes marvelous, but always captivating. His stories reward repeated reading." — Helen Marshall

"One of the best collections I've read in years. Beautifully crafted fiction, stories that'll really affect you and keep you thinking long after you've finished the book." — Tim Lebbon

"The exceptional quality of the writing aside, what most impressed me about this collection was how the uncanny and the supernatural were used to augment stories that a chronicler of everyday tragedy and misfortune, like William Gay for example, often wrote about. At times I felt like I was reading a new approach to horror fiction, and that's a very refreshing prickle to feel across my scalp." — Adam Nevill

"*North American Lake Monsters is* not a physi
and elegant in appearance, not heavy 1
are deceptive. Because it is a truly impr(

T0162984

should be paid. The stories carry (so lightly) a weight of hinterland and incident, of emotional power and implication, seemingly to excess for their modest size. And they punch with that weight solidly behind them."
— John Howard, *Wormwood*

"These are not happy endings. They are sad and unsettling, but always beautifully written with skillful and insightful prose. It is a remarkable collection." —*Hellnotes*

"This is the most striking quality of this extraordinary collection: the compassion of Ballingrud's gaze. He makes no excuses for his characters, never comes near to glorifying their bad choices, and yet never looks down on them. The reader is left with the scarcely bearable knowledge that in the end, the subjects of *North American Lake Monsters* are human."—*Amazing Stories*

"He breathes life into rough, blue-collar characters and places them in some of the best dark fiction being written today. Every single story in this collection is an emotional gut punch. The despair that saturates these tales is rich, and often it is not the supernatural elements in these tales that is horrific." — *Arkham Digest*

"For those willing to go down the dark road that's laid out here, and those willing to feel complex patterns of sympathy, disgust, and horror for (often bad) people, this is an interesting collection. Uncomfortable a read as it is, it has the tinge of reality to it: a reality that often we'd rather not look at."
— Brit Mandelo, Tor.com

"It's Raymond Carver territory. And shattering each story is the luminous, the terrifying, the Lovecraftian otherness that reveals what it really feels like to be alive in this moment in time." — Maureen F. McHugh

"One of the best horror short story collections published during the last couple of years." — *Rising Shadows*

"These stories are dark and gritty nightmares, filled with a deep and humane soulfulness. You don't get a lot of dark fiction or horror quite like that. Wonderful stuff." — Christopher Barzak

# NORTH AMERICAN LAKE MONSTERS

# NORTH AMERICAN LAKE MONSTERS

STORIES

## Nathan Ballingrud

Small Beer Press
Easthampton, MA

*North American Lake Monsters: Stories* copyright © 2013 by Nathan Ballingrud (nathanballingrud.com). All rights
reserved. Page 209 functions as an extenstion of the copyright page.
Cover image "Persian manuscript illumination of Leviathan or Cetus" from Corbis.
*The End of the Affair* copyright © 1951 by Graham Greene. Used by permission of Vintage, a division of
Random House, Inc.

Small Beer Press
150 Pleasant Street #306
Easthampton, MA 01027
smallbeerpress.com
weightlessbooks.com
info@smallbeerpress.com

Distributed to the trade by Consortium.

First Edition       5 6 7 8 9 0

Library of Congress Cataloging-in-Publication Data

Ballingrud, Nathan.
  [Short stories. Selections]
  North American Lake Monsters : Stories / Nathan Ballingrud. -- First Edition.
      pages cm
  ISBN 978-1-61873-059-6 (cloth : alk. paper) -- ISBN 978-1-61873-060-2 (paper : alk. paper) --
ISBN 978-1-61873-061-9 (ebook)
  I. Title.
  PS3602.A623N67 2013
  813'.6--dc23
                        2013016675

Text set in Centaur. Titles in Attic Antique.
Author photo courtesy of Max Cooper.
Printed on 55# Natures Natural 30% PCR Recycled Paper by the Versa Press in East Peoria, IL.

*For Mom and Dad,*
*for Jesse,*
*and for Mia*

# Contents

"I think I had meant to make everything well again, until my victim turned her face, bleary and beautiful with sleep and full of trust, towards me. She had forgotten the quarrel, and I found even in her forgetfulness a new cause. How twisted we humans are, and yet they say a God made us . . ."

Graham Greene, *The End of the Affair*

# You Go Where It Takes You

*He did not look like a man who* would change her life. He was big, roped with muscles from working on offshore oil rigs, and tending to fat. His face was broad and inoffensively ugly, as though he had spent a lifetime taking blows and delivering them. He wore a brown raincoat against the light morning drizzle and against the threat of something more powerful held in abeyance. He breathed heavily, moved slowly, found a booth by the window overlooking the water, and collapsed into it. He picked up a syrup-smeared menu and studied it with his whole attention, like a student deciphering Middle English. He was like every man who ever walked into that diner. He did not look like a beginning or an end.

That day, the Gulf of Mexico and all the earth was blue and still. The little town of Port Fourchon clung like a barnacle to Louisiana's southern coast, and behind it the water stretched into the distance for as many miles as the eye could hold. Hidden by distance were the oil rigs and the workers who supplied the town with its economy. At night she could see their lights, ringing the horizon like candles in a vestibule. Toni's morning shift was nearing its end; the dining area was nearly empty. She liked to spend those slow hours out on the diner's balcony, overlooking the water.

Her thoughts were troubled by the phone call she had received that morning. Gwen, her three-year-old daughter, was offering increasing resistance to the male staffers at the Daylight Daycare, resorting lately to biting them or kicking them in the ribs when they knelt to calm her. Only days before, Toni had been waylaid there by a lurking social worker who talked to her in a gentle saccharine voice, who touched her hand maddeningly and said, "No one is judging you; we just want to help." The social worker had mentioned the word "psychologist" and asked about their home life. Toni had been embarrassed and enraged, and was only able to conclude the interview with a mumbled promise to schedule another one soon. That her daughter was already displaying such grievous signs of social ineptitude stunned Toni, left her feeling hopeless and betrayed.

It also made her think about Donny again, who had abandoned her years ago to move to New Orleans, leaving her a single mother at twenty-three. She wished death on him that morning, staring over the railing at the unrelenting progression of waves. She willed it along the miles and into his heart.

"You know what you want?" she asked.

"Um . . . just coffee." He looked at her breasts and then at her eyes.

"Cream and sugar?"

"No thanks. Just coffee."

"Suit yourself."

The only other customer in the diner was Crazy Claude by the door, speaking conversationally to a cooling plate of scrambled eggs and listening to his radio through his earphones. A tinny roar leaked out around his ears. Pedro, the short-order cook, lounged behind the counter, his big round body encased in layers of soiled white clothing, enthralled by a guitar magazine which he had spread out by the cash register. The kitchen slumbered behind him, exuding a thick fug of onions and burnt frying oil. It would stay mostly dormant until the middle of the week, when the shifts would change on the rigs and tides of men would ebb and flow through the small town.

So when she brought the coffee back to the man, she thought nothing of it when he asked her to join him. She fetched herself a cup of coffee as well and then sat across from him in the booth, grateful to transfer the weight from her feet.

"You ain't got no name tag," he said.

"Oh . . . I guess I lost it somewhere. My name's Toni."

"That's real pretty."

She gave a quick derisive laugh. "The hell it is. It's short for Antoinette."

He held out his hand and said, "I'm Alex."

She took it and they shook. "You work offshore, Alex?"

"Some. I ain't been out there for a while, though." He smiled and gazed into the murk of his coffee. "I've been doing a lot of driving around."

Toni shook loose a cigarette from her pack and lit it. She lied and said, "Sounds exciting."

"I don't guess it is, though. But I bet this place could be, sometimes. I bet you see all kinds of people come through here."

"Well . . . I guess so."

"How long you been here?"

"About three years."

"You like it?"

She felt a flare of anger. "Yeah, Alex, I fucking love it. Who wouldn't?"

"Oh, hey, all right." He held up his hands. "I'm sorry."

She shook her head, immediately ashamed. "No. I'm sorry. I just got a lot on my mind today I guess. This place is fine."

He cocked a half smile. "So why don't you come out with me after work? Maybe I can help distract you." His thick hands were on the table between them. They looked like they could break rocks.

Toni smiled at him. "You known me for what. Five minutes?"

"What can I say. I'm an impulsive guy. Caution to the wind!" He drained his cup in two great swallows, as though to illustrate his recklessness.

"Well, let me go get you some more coffee, Danger Man." She patted his hand as she rose.


It was reckless impulse that brought Donny back to her, briefly, just over a year ago. After a series of phone calls that progressed from petulant to playful to newly curious, he drove back down to Port Fourchon in his disintegrating blue Pinto one Friday afternoon to spend a weekend with them. It was nice at first, though there was no talk of what might happen after Sunday.

Gwen had just started going to daycare. Stunned by the vertiginous growth of the world, she was beset by huge emotions; varieties of rage passed through her little body like weather systems, and no amount of coddling from Toni would settle her.

Although he wouldn't admit it, Toni knew Donny was curious about the baby, that his vanity was satisfied by the knowledge that she would grow to reflect many of his own features and behaviors.

But Gwen refused to participate in generating any kind of mystique that might keep him landed here, revealing herself instead as what Toni knew her to be: a pink, pudgy little assemblage of flesh and ferocity that giggled or raved seemingly without discrimination, that walked without grace and appeared to lack any qualities of beauty or intelligence whatsoever.

The sex with Donny was as good as it had ever been, though, and he didn't seem to mind the baby too much. When he talked about calling in sick to work on Monday, she began to hope for something lasting.

Early Sunday afternoon, they decided to put Gwen to bed early and free up the evening for themselves. First she had to have a bath, and Donny assumed that responsibility with the air of a man handling a volatile explosive. He filled the tub with eight inches of water and plunked her in. He sat back and watched as, with furrowed brow, she went about the serious business of play: dropping the shampoo bottles into the water with her, moving them around like ships at sea. Toni sat on the toilet seat behind him, and it occurred to her that this was her family. She felt buoyant, sated.

Then Gwen rose abruptly from the water and clapped her hands joyously. "Two! Two poops! One, two!"

Aghast, Toni saw two little turds sitting on the bottom of the tub, rolling slightly in the currents generated by Gwen's capering feet. Donny's hand shot out and cuffed his daughter on the side of her head. She fell against the wall and bounced into the water with a terrific splash. And then she screamed. It was the most appalling sound Toni had ever heard in her life.

Toni stared at him, agape. She could not summon the will to move. The baby, sitting on her butt in the soiled water, filled the tiny bathroom with a sound like a bomb siren, and she just wanted her to shut up, shut up, just shut the fuck up.

"Shut up, goddamnit! Shut up!"

Donny looked at her, his face an unreadable mess of confused emotion; he got to his feet and pushed roughly past her. Soon she heard the sound of a door closing. His car started up, and he was gone. She stared at her stricken daughter and tried to quiet the sudden stampeding fury.

She refilled Alex's cup and sat down with him, leaving the pot on the table. She retrieved her cigarette from the ashtray only to discover that it had expired in her absence. "Well, shit," she said.

Alex nodded agreeably. "I'm on the run," he said.

"What?"

"It's true. I'm on the run. I stole a car."

Alarmed, Toni looked out the window, but the parking lot was on the other side of the diner. All she could see from here was the Gulf. "Why are you telling me this? I don't want to know this."

"It's a station wagon. I can't believe it even runs anymore. I was in Morgan City, and I had to get out fast. The car was right there. I took it."

He had a manic look in his eye, and although he was smiling, he seemed agitated; his fingers tapped the table, the cords in his hands standing out like cables. She felt a growing disquiet coupled with a mounting excitement. He was dangerous, this man. He was a falling hammer.

"I don't think that guy over there likes me," he said.

"What?" She turned and saw Crazy Claude in stasis, staring at Alex. His jaw was cantilevered in mid chew. "That's just Claude," she said. "He's all right."

Alex was still smiling, but it had taken on a different character, one she couldn't place and which set loose a strange, giddy feeling inside her. "No, I think it's me. He keeps looking over here."

"Really, Claude's okay. He's harmless as a kitten."

"I want to show you something." Alex reached inside his rain-coat, and for a moment Toni thought he was going to pull out a gun and start shooting. She felt no inclination to move; she waited for what would come. Instead, he withdrew a crumpled Panama hat. It had been considerably crushed to fit into his pocket, and once freed it began to unfold itself, like something blooming.

She looked at it. "It's a hat," she said.

He stared at it like he expected it to lurch across the table with some hideous agenda. "That's an object of terrible power," he said.

"Alex—it's a hat. It's a thing you put on your head."

"It belongs to the man I stole the car from. Here," he said, push-ing it across to her. "Put it on."

She did. She was growing tired of the serious turn he seemed to have taken and decided to be a little playful. She turned her chin to her shoulder and pouted her lips, looking at him out of the corner of her eye, like she thought a model might.

He smiled. "Who are you?"

"I'm a supermodel."

"What's your name? Where are you from?"

She affected a light, breathy voice. "My name is Violet, I'm from L.A., and I'm strutting down a catwalk wearing this hat and nothing else. Everybody loves me and is taking my picture."

She laughed self-consciously; he was leaning over the table toward her and smiling. She could see the tip of his tongue between his teeth. He just watched her for a second. "See? It's powerful. You can be anybody."

She gave the hat back, feeling suddenly deflated. It was as though by saying it, he'd broken the spell. "I don't know," she said.

"You know," Alex said, "the guy I stole the car from was something of a thief himself, it turns out. You should see what he left in there."

"Why don't you show me?"

He smiled again, and glanced at the nearly empty diner. "Now?"

"No. In half an hour. When I get off work."

"But it's all packed up. I don't let that stuff just fly around loose."

"Then you can show me at my place."

And so it was decided. She got up and went about preparing for the next shift, which consisted of restocking a few ketchup packets and starting a fresh pot of coffee. She refilled Crazy Claude's cup and gave him another ten packets of sugar, all of which he methodically opened and dumped into his drink. When her relief arrived, Toni hung her apron by the waitress station and collected Alex on her way to the door.

"We have to stop by the daycare and pick up my kid," she said.

If this news fazed him, he didn't show it.

As they passed Claude's table they heard a distant, raucous sound coming from his earphones.

Alex curled his lip. "Idiot. How does he hear himself think?"

"He doesn't. That's the point. He hears voices in his head. He plays the radio loud so he can drown them out."

"You're kidding me."

"Nope."

Alex stopped and turned around, regarding the back of Claude's head with renewed interest. "How many people does he have in there?"

"I never asked."

"Well, holy shit."

Outside, the sun was setting, the day beginning to cool down. The rain had stopped at some point, and the world glowed with a bright, wet sheen. They decided that he would follow her in his car. It was a rusty old battlewagon from the Seventies; several boxes were piled in the back. She paid them no attention.

She knew, when they stepped into her little apartment, that they would wind up making love, and she found herself wondering what it would be like. She watched him move, noted the graceful articulation of his body, the careful restraint he displayed in her living room, which was filled with fragile things. She saw the skin beneath his clothing, watched it stretch and move.

"Don't worry," she said, touching the place between his shoulder blades. "You won't break nothing."

About Gwen there was more doubt. Unleashed like a darting fish into the apartment, she was gone with a bright squeal, away from the strange new man around whom she had been so quiet and doleful, into the dark grottoes of her home.

"It's real pretty," Alex said.

"A bunch a knickknacks mostly. Nothing special."

He shook his head like he did not believe it. Her apartment was decorated mostly with the inherited flotsam of her grandmother's life: bland wall hangings, beaten old furniture which had hosted too many bodies spreading gracelessly into old age, and a vast and silly collection of glass figurines: leaping dolphins and sleeping dragons and such. It was all meant to be homey and reassuring, but it just reminded her of how far away she was from the life she really wanted. It seemed like a desperate construct, and she hated it very much.

For now, Alex made no mention of the objects in his car or the hat in his pocket. He appeared to be more interested in Gwen, who was peering around the corner of the living room and regarding him with a suspicious and hungry eye, who seemed to intuit that from this large alien figure on her mama's couch would come mighty upheavals.

He was a man—that much Gwen knew immediately—and therefore a dangerous creature. He would make her mama behave unnaturally; maybe even cry. He was too big, like the giant in her storybook. She wondered if he ate children. Or mamas.

Mama was sitting next to him.

"Come here, Mama." She slapped her thigh like Mama did when she wanted Gwen to pay attention to her. Maybe she could lure Mama away from the giant, and they could wait in the closet until he got bored and went away. "Come here, Mama, come here."

"Go on and play now, Gwen."

"No! Come here!"

"She don't do too well around men," said Mama.

"That's okay," said the giant. "These days I don't either." He patted the cushion next to him. "Come over here, baby. Let me say hi."

Gwen, alarmed at this turn of events, retreated a step behind a corner. They were in the living room, which had her bed in it, and her toys. Behind her, Mama's darkened room yawned like a throat. She sat between the two places, wrapped her arms around her knees, and waited.

⚘

"She's so afraid," Alex said after she retreated from view. "You know why?"

"Um, because you're big and scary?"

"Because she already knows about possibilities. Long as you know there are options in life, you get scared of choosing the wrong one."

Toni leaned away from him and gave him a mistrustful smile. "Okay, Einstein. Easy with the philosophy."

"No, really. She's like a thousand different people right now, all waiting to be, and every time she makes a choice, one of those people goes away forever. Until finally you run out of choices and you are whoever you are. She's afraid of what she'll lose by coming out to see me. Of who she'll never get to be."

Toni thought of her daughter and saw nothing but a series of shut doors. "Are you drunk?"

"What? You know I ain't drunk."

"Stop talking like you are, then. I've had enough of that shit to last me my whole life."

"Jesus, I'm sorry."

"Forget it." Toni got up and rounded the corner to scoop up her daughter. "I got to bathe her and put her to bed. If you want to wait, it's up to you."

She carried Gwen into the bathroom and began the nightly ministrations. She felt Donny's presence too strongly tonight, and Alex's sophomoric philosophizing sounded just like him when he'd had too many beers. She found herself halfway hoping that the obligations of motherhood would bore Alex, and that he would leave. She listened for the sound of the front door.

Instead, she heard footsteps behind her and felt his heavy hand on her shoulder. It squeezed her gently, and his big body settled down beside her. He said something kind to Gwen and brushed a strand of wet hair from her eyes. Toni felt something move slowly in her chest, subtly yet with powerful effect, like Atlas rolling a shoulder.

Gwen suddenly shrieked and collapsed into the water, sending a surge of water over them both. Alex reached in to stop her from knocking her head against the porcelain and received a kick in the mouth for his troubles. Toni shouldered him aside and jerked her out of the tub. She hugged her daughter tightly to her chest and whispered motherly incantations into her ear. After a brief struggle, Gwen finally settled into her mother's embrace and whimpered quietly, turning her whole focus onto the warm, familiar hand rubbing her back, up and down, up and down, until, finally, her energy flagged, and she drifted into a tentative sleep.

When Gwen was dressed and in her bed, Toni turned her attention to Alex. "Here, let's clean you up."

She steered him back into the bathroom. She opened the shower curtain and pointed to the soap and the shampoo and said, "It smells kind of flowery, but it gets the job done," and the whole time he was looking at her, and she thought: So this is it; this is how it happens.

"Help me," he said, lifting his arms over his head. She smiled wanly and began to undress him. She watched his body as she unwrapped it, and when he was naked she pressed herself against him and ran her fingers over his skin.

Later, when they were in bed together, she said, "I'm sorry about tonight."

"She's just a kid."

"No, I mean about snapping at you. I don't know why I did."

"It's okay."

"I just don't like to think about what could have been. There's no point to it. Sometimes I think a person doesn't have much to say about what happens to them anyway."

"I really don't know."

She stared out the little window across from the bed and watched slate gray clouds skim across the sky. Behind them were the stars.

NATHAN BALLINGRUD

"Ain't you gonna tell me why you stole a car?"

"I had to."

"But why?"

He was silent for a little while. "It don't matter," he said.

"If you don't tell me, it makes me think you mighta killed somebody."

"Maybe I did."

She thought about that for a minute. It was too dark to see anything in the bedroom, but she scanned her eyes across it anyway, knowing the location of every piece of furniture, every worn tube of lipstick and leaning stack of lifestyle magazines. She could see through the walls and feel the sagging weight of the figurines on the shelves. She tried to envision each one in turn, as though searching for one that would act as a talisman against this subject and the weird celebration it raised in her.

"Did you hate him?"

"I don't hate anybody," he said. "I wish I did. I wish I had it in me."

"Come on, Alex. You're in my house. You got to tell me something."

After a long moment, he said, "The guy I stole the car from. I call him Mr. Gray. I never saw him, except in dreams. I don't know anything about him, really. But I don't think he's human. And I know he's after me."

"What do you mean?"

"I have to show you." Without another word, he got to his feet and pulled on his jeans. She could sense a mounting excitement in his demeanor, and it inspired a similar feeling in herself. She followed him out of her bedroom, pulling a long T-shirt over her head as she went. Gwen slept deeply in the living room; they stepped over her mattress on the way out.

The grass was wet under their bare feet, the air heavy with the salty smell of the sea. Alex's car was parked at the curb, hugging the ground like a great beetle. He opened the rear hatch and pulled the closest box toward them.

"Look," he said, and opened the box.

At first, Toni could not comprehend what she was seeing. She thought it was a cat lying on a stack of tan leather jackets, but that wasn't right, and only when Alex grabbed a handful of the cat and pulled it out did she realize that it was human hair. Alex lifted the whole object out of the box, and she found herself staring at what appeared to be the tanned and cured hide of a human being, dark empty holes in its face like some rubber Halloween mask.

"I call this one Willie, 'cause he's so well hung," said Alex, and offered an absurd laugh.

Toni fell back a step.

"But there's women in here too, all kinds of people. I counted ninety-six. All carefully folded." He offered the skin to Toni, but when she made no move to touch it he started to fold it up again. "I guess there ain't no reason to see them all. You get the idea."

"Alex, I want to go back inside."

"Okay, just hang on a second."

She waited while he closed the lid of the box and slid it back into place. With the hide tucked under one arm, he shut the hatch, locked it, and turned to face her. He was grinning, bouncing on the balls of his feet. "Okeydokey," he said, and they headed back indoors.

They returned quietly to the bedroom, stepping softly to avoid waking Gwen.

"Did you kill all those people?" Toni asked when the door was closed.

"What? Didn't you hear me? I stole a car. That's what was in it."

"Mr. Gray's car."

"That's right."

"Who is he? What are they for?" she asked; but she already knew what they were for.

"They're alternatives," he said. "They're so you can be somebody else."

She thought about that. "Have you worn any of them?"

"One. I haven't got up the balls to do it again yet." He reached into the front pocket of his jeans and withdrew a leather sheath. From it he pulled a small, ugly little knife that looked like an eagle's talon. "You got to take off the one you're wearing, first. It hurts."

Toni swallowed. The sound was thunderous in her ears. "Where's your first skin? The one you was born with?"

Alex shrugged. "I threw that one out. I ain't like Mr. Gray. I don't know how to preserve them. Besides, what do I want to keep it for? I must not have liked it too much in the first place, right?"

She felt a tear accumulate in the corner of her eye and willed it not to fall. She was afraid and exhilarated. "Are you going to take mine?"

Alex looked startled, then seemed to remember he was holding the knife. He put it back in its sheath. "I told you, baby, I'm not the one who killed those people. I don't need any more than what's already there." She nodded, and the tear streaked down her face. He touched it away with the back of his fingers. "Hey now," he said.

She grabbed his hand. "Where's mine?" She gestured at the skin folded beside him. "I want one, too. I want to come with you."

"Oh, Jesus, no, Toni. You can't."

"But why not? Why can't I go?"

"Come on now, you got a family here."

"It's just me and her. That ain't no family."

"You have a little girl, Toni. What's wrong with you? That's your life now." He stepped out of his pants and, naked, pulled the knife from its sheath. "I can't argue about this. I'm going now. I'm gonna change first, though, so you might not want to watch." She made no move to leave. He paused, considering something. "I got to ask you something," he said. "I been wondering about this lately. Do you think it's possible for something beautiful to come out of an awful thing? Do you think a good life can redeem a horrible act?"

"Of course I do," she said quickly, sensing some second chance here, if only she said the right words. "Yes."

Alex touched the blade to his scalp just above his right ear and drew it in an arc over the crown of his head until it reached his left ear. Bright red blood crept down from his hairline in a slow tide, sending rivulets and tributaries along his jaw and his throat, hanging from his eyelashes like raindrops from flower petals. "God, I really hope so," he said. He worked his fingers into the incision and began to tug.

Watching the skin fall away from him, she was reminded of nothing so much as a butterfly struggling into daylight.


She is driving west on I-10. The morning sun, which has just breached the horizon, flares in her rearview mirror. Port Fourchon is far behind her, and the Texas border looms. Beside her, Gwen is sitting on the floor of the passenger seat, playing with the Panama hat Alex left behind when he drove north. Toni has never seen the need for a car seat. Gwen is happier moving about on her own, and in times like this, when Toni feels a slow, crawling anger in her blood, the last thing she needs is a temper tantrum from her daughter.

After he left, she was faced with a few options. She could put on her stupid pink uniform, take Gwen to daycare, and go back to work. She could drive up to New Orleans and find Donny. Or she could say fuck it all and just get in the car and drive, aimlessly and free of expectation, which is what she is doing.

She cries for the first dozen miles or so, and it is such a luxury that she just lets it come, feeling no guilt.

Gwen, still feeling the dregs of sleep, as yet undecided whether to be cranky for being awakened early or excited by the trip, pats her on the leg. "You okay, Mama, you okay?"

"Yes, baby. Mama's okay."

Toni sees the sign she has been looking for coming up on the side of the road. Rest Stop, 2 miles.

When they get there, she pulls in, coming to a stop in an empty lot. Gwen climbs up in the seat and peers out the window. She sees the warm red glow of a Coke machine and decides that she will be happy today, that waking up early means excitement and the possibility of treats.

"Have the Coke, Mama? Have it, have the Coke?"

"Okay, sweetie."

They get out and walk up to the Coke machine. Gwen laughs happily and slaps it several times, listening to the distant dull echo inside. Toni puts in some coins and grabs the tumbling can. She cracks it open and gives it to her daughter, who takes it delightedly.

"Coke!"

"That's right." Toni kneels beside her as Gwen takes several ambitious swigs. "Gwen? Honey? Mama's got to go potty, okay? You stay right here, okay? Mama will be right back."

Gwen lowers the can, a little overwhelmed by the cold blast of carbonation, and nods her head. "Right back!"

"That's right, baby."

Toni starts away. Gwen watches her mama as she heads back to the car and climbs in. She shuts the door and starts the engine. Gwen takes another drink of Coke. The car pulls away from the curb, and she feels a bright stab of fear. But Mama said she was coming right back, so she will wait right here.

Toni turns the wheel and speeds back out onto the highway. There is no traffic in sight. The sign welcoming her to Texas flashes by and is gone. She presses the accelerator. Her heart is beating.

# Wild Acre

*Three men are lying in what will someday* be a house. For now it's just a skeleton of beams and supports standing amid the foundations and frames of other burgeoning houses in a large, bulldozed clearing. The earth around them is a churned, orange clay. Forest abuts the Wild Acre development site, crawling up the side of the Blue Ridge Mountains, hickory and maple hoarding darkness as the sky above them shades into deepening blue. The hope is that soon there will be finished buildings here, and then more skeletons and more houses, with roads to navigate them. But now there are only felled trees, and mud, and these naked frames. And three men, lying on a cold wooden floor, staring up through the roof beams as the sky organizes a nightfall. They have a cooler packed with beer and a baseball bat.

Several yards away, mounted in the back of Jeremy's truck, is a hunting rifle.

Jeremy watches stars burn into life: first two, then a dozen. He came here hoping for violence, but the evening has softened him. Lying on his back, balancing a beer on the great swell of his belly, he hopes there will be no occasion for it. Wild Acre is abandoned for now, and might be for a long time to come, making it an easy target. Three nights over the past week, someone has come onto the work site and committed small but infuriating acts of vandalism: stealing and damaging tools and equipment, spray-painting vulgar images on the project manager's trailer, even taking a dump on the floor of one of the unfinished houses. The project manager complained to the police, but with production stalled and bank accounts running dry, angry subcontractors and prospective homeowners consumed most of his attention. The way Jeremy saw it, it was up to the trade guys to protect the site. He figured the vandals for environmental activists, pissed that their mountain had been shaved for this project; he worried that they'd soon start burning down his frames. Insurance would cover the developer, but he and his company would go bankrupt. So he's come here with Dennis and Renaldo—his best friend and his most able brawler, respectively—hoping to catch them in the act and beat them into the dirt.

"They're not coming tonight," says Renaldo.

"No shit," says Dennis. "You think it's 'cause you talk too loud?" Dennis has been with Jeremy ten years now. For a while, Jeremy thought about making him partner, but the man just couldn't keep his shit together, and Jeremy privately nixed the idea. Dennis is forty-eight years old, ten years older than Jeremy. His whole life is invested in this work: he's a carpenter and nothing else. He has three young children, and talks about having more. This work stoppage threatens to impoverish him. "Bunch of goddamn Green Party eco-fucking-terrorist motherfuckers," Dennis says.

Jeremy watches him. Dennis is moving his jaw around, working himself into a rage. That would be useful if he thought anybody was going to show tonight; but he thinks they've screwed it all up. They got here too early, before the sun was down, and they made too much noise. No one will come now.

"Dude. Grab yourself a beer and mellow out."

"These kids are fucking with my *life*, man! You tell me to mellow out?"

"Dennis, man, you're not the only one." A breeze comes down the mountain and washes over them. Jeremy feels it move through his hair, deepening his sense of easy contentment. He remembers feeling that rage just this afternoon, talking to that asshole from the bank, and he knows he'll feel it again. He knows he'll have to. But right now it's as distant and alien as the full moon, catching fire unknown miles above them. "But they're not here. 'Naldo's right, we blew it. We'll come back tomorrow night." He looks into the forest crowding against the development site and wonders why they didn't think to hide themselves there. "And we'll do it right. So for tonight? Just chill."

Renaldo leans over and claps Dennis on the back. "Mañana, amigo. Mañana!"

Jeremy knows that Renaldo's optimism is one of the reasons Dennis resents him, but the young Mexican wouldn't be able to function in this all-white crew without it. He gets a lot of crap from these guys and just takes it. When work is this hard to come by, pride is a luxury. Nevertheless Jeremy is dismayed at Renaldo's easy manner in the face of it all. A man can't endure that kind of diminishment, he thinks, and not release anger somewhere.

Dennis casts Jeremy a defeated look. The sky retains a faint glow from twilight, but darkness has settled over the ground. The men are black shapes. "It's not the same for you, man. Your wife works, you know? You got another income. My wife don't do *shit*."

"That's not just her fault, though, Dennis. What would you do if Rebecca told you she was getting a job tomorrow?"

"I'd say it's about goddamned time!"

Jeremy laughs. "Bullshit. You'd just knock her up again. If that woman went out into the world you'd lose your mind, and you know it."

Dennis shakes his head, but a sort of smile breaks through.

The conversation has undermined whatever small good the beer has done for him tonight: all the old fears are stirring. He hasn't been able to pay these men for three weeks now, and even an old friend like Dennis will have to move on eventually. The business hasn't paid a bill in months, and Tara's teacher's salary certainly isn't enough to support them by itself. He realizes that their objective tonight is mostly just an excuse to vent some anger; cracking some misguided kids' heads isn't going to get the bank to stop calling him, and it isn't going to get the bulldozers moving again. It isn't going to let him call his crew and tell them they can come back to work, either.

But he won't let it get to him tonight. Not this beautiful, moonlit night on the mountain, with bare wood lifting skyward all around them. "Fuck it," he says, and claps his hands twice, a reclining sultan. "'Naldo! Más cervezas!"

Renaldo, who has just settled onto his back, slowly folds himself into a sitting position. He climbs to his feet and heads to the cooler without complaint. He's accustomed to being the gofer.

"Little Mexican bastard," Dennis says. "I bet he's got fifty cousins packed into a trailer he's trying to support."

"Hablo fucking inglés, motherfucker," Renaldo says.

"What? Speak English! I can't understand you."

Jeremy laughs. They drink more beer, and the warmth of it washes through their bodies until they are illuminated, three little candles in a clearing, surrounded by the dark woods.


Jeremy says, "I gotta take a piss, dude." The urge has been building in him for some time, but he's been lying back on the floor, his body filled with a warm, beery lethargy, and he's been reluctant to move. Now it manifests as a sudden, urgent pain, sufficient to propel him to his feet and across the red clay road. The wind has risen and the forest is a wall of dark sound, the trees no longer distinct from each other but instead a writhing movement, a grasping energy which prickles his skin and hurries his step. The moon, which only a short while ago seemed a kindly lantern in the dark, smolders in the sky. Behind him, Dennis and Renaldo continue some wandering conversation, and he holds on to the sound of their voices to ward off a sudden, inexplicable rising fear. He casts a glance back toward the house. The ground inclines toward it, and at this angle he can't see either of them. Just the cross-gables shouldering into the sky.

He steps into the tree line, going back a few feet for modesty's sake. Situating himself behind a tree, he opens his fly and lets loose. The knot of pain in his gut starts to unravel.

Walking around has lit up the alcohol in his blood, and he's starting to feel angry again. If I don't get to hit somebody soon, he thinks, I'm going to snap. I'm going to unload on somebody that doesn't deserve it. If Dennis opens his whining mouth one more time it might be him.

Jeremy feels a twinge of remorse at the thought; Dennis is one of those guys who has to talk about his fears, or they'll eat him alive. He has to give a running commentary on every grim possibility, as if by voicing a fear he'd chase it into hiding. Jeremy relates more to Renaldo, who has yet to utter one frustrated thought about how long it's been since he's been paid, or what their future prospects might be. He doesn't really know Renaldo, knows his personal situation even less, and something about that strikes him as proper. The idea of a man keening in pain has always embarrassed him.

When Jeremy has weak moments, he saves them for private expression. Even Tara, who has been a rock of optimism throughout all of this, isn't privy to them. She's a smart, intuitive woman, though, and Jeremy recognizes his fortune in her. She assures him that he is both capable and industrious, and that he can find work other than hammering nails into wood, should it come down to it. She's always held the long view. He feels a sudden swell of love for her, as he stands there pissing there in the woods: a desperate, childlike need. He blinks rapidly, clearing his eyes.

He's staring absently into the forest as he thinks this all through, and so it takes him a few moments to focus his gaze and realize that someone is staring back at him.

It's a young man—a kid, really—several feet deeper into the forest, obscured by low growth and hanging branches and darkness.

He's skinny and naked. Smiling at him. Just grinning like a jack-o'-lantern.

"Oh, shit!"

Jeremy lurches from the tree, yanking frantically at his zipper, which has caught on the denim of his pants. He staggers forward a step, his emotions a snarl of rage, excitement, and humiliation. "What the fuck!" he shouts. The kid bounds to his right and disappears, soundlessly.

"Dennis? Dennis! They're here!"

He turns but he can't see up the hill. The angle is bad. All he can see through the trees is the pale wooden frame standing out against the sky like bones, and he's taking little hopping steps as he wrestles with his zipper. He trips over a root and crashes painfully to the ground.

He hears Dennis's raised voice.

He climbs awkwardly to his feet. The zipper finally comes free and Jeremy yanks it up, running clumsily through the branches while fastening his fly. As he ascends the small incline and crosses the muddy road he can discern shapes wrestling between the wooden support struts; he hears them fighting, hears the brute explosions of breath and the heavy impact of colliding meat. It sounds like the kid is putting up a pretty good fight; Jeremy wants to get in on the action before it's all over. He's overcome by instinct and violent impulse.

He's exalted by it.

A voice breaks out of the tumult and it's so warped by anguish that it takes him a moment to recognize it as Dennis's scream.

Jeremy jerks to a stop. He burns crucial seconds trying to understand what he's heard.

And then he hears something else: a heavy tearing, like ripping canvas, followed by a liquid sound of dropped weight, of moist, heavy objects sliding to the ground. He catches a glimpse of motion, something huge and fast in the house, and then an inverted leg standing out suddenly like a dark rip in the bright flank of stars, and then nothing.

A high, keening wail—ephemeral, barely audible—rises from the unfinished house like a wisp of smoke.

Finally he reaches the top of the hill and looks inside.

Dennis is on his back, his body frosted by moonlight. He's lifting his head, staring down at himself. Organs are strewn to one side of his body like beached, black jellyfish, dark blood pumping slowly from the gape in his belly and spreading around him in a gory nimbus. His head drops back and he lifts it again. Renaldo is on his back too, arms flailing, trying to hold off the thing bestride him: huge, black-furred, dog-begotten, its man-like fingers wrapped around Renaldo's face and pushing his head into the floor so hard that the wood cracks beneath it. It lifts its shaggy head, bloody ropes of drool swinging from its snout and arcing into the moonsilvered night. It peels its lips from its teeth. Renaldo's screams are muffled beneath its hand.

"Shoot it," Dennis says. His voice is calm, like he's suggesting coffee. "Shoot it, Jeremy."

The house swings out of sight and the road scrolls by, lurching and violently tilting, and Jeremy realizes with some dismay that he is running. His truck, a small white pick-up, is less than fifty feet away. Parked just beyond it is Renaldo's little import, its windows rolled down, rosary beads hanging from the rearview mirror.

Jeremy runs fill-tilt into the side of his truck, rebounding off it and almost falling to the ground. He opens the door and is inside with what feels like unnatural speed. He slides across to the driver's side and digs into his pocket for the keys, fingers grappling furiously through change and crumpled receipts until he finds them.

He can feel the rifle mounted on the rack behind his head, radiating a monstrous energy. It's loaded; it's always loaded.

He looks through the passenger window and sees something stand upright inside the frames, looking back at him. He sees Renaldo spasming beneath it. He sees the dark forested mountains looming behind this stillborn community with a hostile intelligence. He guns the engine and slams down the accelerator, turning the wheel hard to the left. The tires spray mud in huge arcs until they find traction, and he speeds down the hill toward the highway. The truck bounces hard on the rough path and briefly goes airborne. The engine screams, the sound of it filling his head.

"What the hell are you *looking* at?"

"What?" Jeremy blinked, and looked at his wife.

Breakfast time at the Blue Plate was always busy, but today the noise and the crowd were unprecedented. People crowded on the bench by the door, waiting for a chance to sit down. Short-order cooks and servers hollered at each other over the din of loud customers, boiling fryers, and crackling griddles. He knew that Tara hated it here, but on bad days—and he's had plenty of bad days in the six months since the attack—he needed to be in places like this. Even now, wedged into a booth too narrow for him, with the table's edge pressing uncomfortably into his gut, he did not want to leave.

His attention was drawn by the new busboy. He was young and gangly, lanky hair swinging over his lowered face. He scurried from empty table to empty table, loading dirty plates and coffee mugs into his gray bus tub. He moved with a strange grace through the crowd, like someone well practiced at avoidance. Jeremy was bothered that he couldn't get a clear view of his face.

"Why do you think he wears his hair like that?" he said. "He looks like a drug addict or something. I'm surprised they let him."

Tara rolled her eyes, not even bothering to look. "The busboy? Are you serious?"

"What do you mean?"

"Are you even *listening* to me?"

"What? Of course. Come on." He forced his attention back where it belonged. "You're talking about that guy who teaches the smart kids. What's his name. Tim."

Tara let her stare linger a moment before pressing on. "Yeah, I mean, what an asshole, right? He knows I'm married!"

"Well, that's the attraction."

"The fact that I'm married to you is why he wants me? Oh my God, and I thought *he* had an ego!"

"No, I mean, you're hot, he'd be into you anyway. But the fact that you belong to somebody just adds another incentive. It's a challenge."

"Wait."

"Some guys just like to take what isn't theirs."

"Wait. I *belong* to you now?"

He smiled. "Well . . . yeah, bitch."

She laughed. "You are so lucky we're in a public place right now."

"You're not scary."

"Oh, I'm pretty scary."

"Then how come you can't scare off little Timmy?"

She gave him an exasperated look. "Do you think I'm not trying? He just doesn't care. I think he thinks I'm flirting with him or something. I want him to see you at the Christmas party. Get all alpha male on him. Squeeze his hand really hard when you shake it or something."

A waitress arrived at their table and unloaded their breakfast: fruit salad and a scrambled egg for Tara, a mound of buttery pancakes for Jeremy. Tara cast a critical eye over his plate and said, "We gotta work on that diet of yours, big man. There's a new year coming up. Resolution time."

"Like hell," he said, tucking in. "This is my fuel. I need it if I'm going to defeat Tim in bloody combat."

The sentence hung awkwardly between them. Jeremy found himself staring at her, the stupid smile on his face frozen into something miserable and strange. His scalp prickled, and he felt his face go red.

"Well, that was dumb," he said.

She put her hand over his. "Honey."

He pulled away. "Whatever." He forked some of the pancakes into his mouth, staring down at his plate.

He breathed in deeply, taking in the close, burnt-oil odor of the place, trying to displace the smell of blood and fear which welled up inside him as though he was on the mountain again, half a year ago, watching his friends die in the rearview mirror. He looked around again to see if he could get a look at that creepy busboy's face, but he couldn't spot him in the crowd.

The coroner had decided that a wolf had killed Dennis and Renaldo. It was a big story in the local news for a week or so; there weren't supposed to be any wolves in this part of North Carolina. Nevertheless, the bite marks and the tracks in the mud were clear. Hunting parties had ranged into the woods; they'd bagged a few coyotes, but no wolves. The developer of Wild Acre filed for bankruptcy: buyers who had signed conditional agreements refused to close on the houses, and the banks gave up on the project, locking their coffers for good. Wild Acre became a ghost town of empty house frames and mud. Jeremy's outfit went under, too. He broke the news to his employees and began the dreary process of appeasing his creditors. Tara still pulled down her teacher's salary, but it was barely enough to keep pace, let alone catch them up. They weren't sure how much longer they could afford their own house.

Within a month of the attack, Jeremy discovered that he was unemployable. Demand for his services had dried up. The framing companies were streamlining their payrolls, and nobody wanted to add an expensive ex-owner to their rosters.

He never told his wife what really happened that night. Publicly, he corroborated the coroner's theory, and he tried as best he could to convince himself of it, too. But the thing that had straddled his friend and then stared him down had not been a wolf.

He could not call it by its name.

*L♥*

In the middle of all that were the funerals.

Renaldo's had been a small, cheap affair. He'd felt like an imposter there, too close to the tumultuous emotion on display. Renaldo's mother filled the room with her cries. Jeremy felt alarmed and even a little appalled at her lack of self-consciousness, which was so at odds with her late son's unflappable nature. Everyone spoke in Spanish, and he was sure they were all talking about him. On some level he knew this was ridiculous, but he couldn't shake it.

A young man approached him, late teens or early twenties, dressed in an ill-fitting, rented suit, his hands hanging stiffly at his sides.

Jeremy nodded at him. "Hola," he said. He felt awkward and stupid.

"Hello," the man said. "You were his boss?"

"Yeah, yeah. I'm, um . . . I'm sorry. He was a great worker. You know, one of my best. The guys really liked him. If you knew my guys, you'd know that meant something." He realized he was beginning to ramble, and made himself stop talking.

"Thank you."

"Were you brothers?"

"Brothers-in-law. Married to my sister?"

"Oh, of course." Jeremy didn't know Renaldo had been married. He looked across the gathered crowd, thinking for one absurd moment that he might know her by sight.

"Listen," the man said, "I know you're having some hard times. The business and everything."

Well, here it comes, Jeremy thought. He tried to cut him off at the pass. "I still owed some money to Renaldo. I haven't forgotten. I'll get it to you as soon as I can. I promise."

"To Carmen."

"Of course. To Carmen."

"That's good." He nodded, looking at the ground. Jeremy could sense there was more coming, and he wanted to get away before it arrived. He opened his mouth to express a final platitude before taking his leave, but the young man spoke first. "Why didn't you shoot it?"

He felt something grow cold inside him. "What?"

"I know why you were there. Renaldo told me what was happening. The vandals? He said you had a rifle."

Jeremy bristled. "Listen, I don't know what Renaldo thought, but we weren't going up there to shoot anybody. We were going to scare them. That's all. The gun's in my truck because I'm a hunter. I don't use it to threaten kids."

"But it wasn't kids on the mountain that night, was it?"

They stared at each other for a moment. Jeremy's face was flushed, and he could hear the laboring of his own breath. By contrast the young man seemed entirely at ease; either he didn't really care about why Jeremy didn't shoot that night or he already knew that the answer wouldn't satisfy him.

"No, I guess it wasn't."

"It was a wolf, right?"

Jeremy was silent.

"A wolf?"

He had to moisten his mouth. "Yeah."

"So why didn't you shoot it?"

". . . It happened really fast," he said. "I was out in the woods. I was too late."

Renaldo's brother-in-law gave no reaction, holding his gaze for a few more moments and then nodding slightly. He took a deep breath, turned to look behind him at the others gathered for the funeral, some of whom were staring in their direction. Then he turned back to Jeremy and said, "Thank you for coming. But maybe now, you know, you should go. It's hard for some people to see you."

"Yeah. Okay. Of course." Jeremy backed up a step, and said, "I'm really sorry."

"Okay."

And then he left, grateful to get away, but nearly overwhelmed by shame. He'd removed the rifle from his truck the day after the attack, stowing it in the attic. Its presence was an indictment. Despite what he'd told Renaldo's brother-in-law, he didn't know why he hadn't taken the gun, climbed back out of the truck, and blown the wolf to hell. Because that's all it had been. A wolf. A stupid animal. How many animals had he killed with that very rifle?

Dennis's funeral had been different. There, he was treated like family, if a somewhat distant and misunderstood relation. Rebecca, obese and unemployed, looked doomed as she stood graveside with her three children, completely unanchored from the only person in the world who had cared about her fate, or the fates of those stunned boys at her side. He wanted to apologize to her but he didn't know precisely how, so instead he hugged her after the services and shook the boys' hands and said, "If there's anything I can do."

She wrapped him in a hug.

"Oh, Jeremy," she said.


The boy is skinny and naked. Smiling at him, his teeth shining like cut crystal. Jeremy's pants are unfastened and loose around his hips. He's afraid that if he runs they'll fall and trip him up. The kid can't even be out of high school yet: Jeremy knows he can break him in half if he can just get his hands on him in time. But it's already too late; terror pins him there, and he can only watch. The kid's body begins to shake, and what he thought was a smile is only a rictus of pain—his mouth splits along his cheeks and something loud breaks inside him, cracking like a tree branch. The boy's bowels spray blood and his body convulses like he's in the grip of a seizure.

"Jeremy!"

He opened his eyes. He was in their bedroom, with Tara standing over him. The light was on. The bed felt warm and damp.

"Get out of bed. You had a nightmare."

"Why is the bed all wet?"

She pulled him by his shoulder. She had a strange expression: distracted, pinched. "Come on," she said. "You had an accident."

"What?" He sat up, smelling urine. "What?"

"Get out of bed, please. I have to change the sheets."

He did as she asked. His legs were sticky, his boxers soaked.

Tara began yanking the sheets off the bed as quickly as she could. She tugged the mattress pad off too, and cursed quietly when she saw that the stain had already bled down to the mattress itself.

"Let me help," he said.

"You should get in the shower. I'll take care of this."

". . . I'm sorry."

She turned on him. For a moment he saw the anger and the impatience there, and he was conscious of how long she had been putting up with his stoic routine, of the extent to which she had fastened down her own frustration for the sake of his wounded ego. It threatened to finally spill over, but she pulled it back, she sucked it in for him one more time. Her expression softened. She touched his cheek. "It's okay, baby." She pushed the hair from his forehead, turning the gesture into a caress. "Go ahead and get in the shower, okay?"

"Okay." He headed for the bathroom.

He stripped and got under the hot water. Six months of being without work had caused him to get even heavier, a fact he was acutely conscious of as he lowered himself to the floor and wrapped his arms around his knees. He did not want Tara to see him. He wanted to barricade the door, to wrap barbed wire around the whole room. But fifteen minutes later she joined him there, putting her arms around him and pulling him close, resting her head against his.


Two months after the funeral, Dennis's wife had called and asked him to come over. He arrived at her house—a single-story, three-bedroom bungalow—later that afternoon and was dismayed to see boxes in the living room and the kitchen. The kids, ranging in age from five to thirteen, moved ineffectively among them, piling things in with no regard to maximizing their space or gauging how heavy they might become. Rebecca was a dervish of industry, sliding through the mazes of boxes and furniture with a surprising grace, barking orders at her kids and even at her herself. When she saw him through the screen door, standing on her front porch, she stopped, and in doing so seemed to lose all of her will to move. The boys stopped too, and followed her gaze out to him.

"Becca, what's going on?"

"What's it look like? I'm packin boxes." She turned her back to him and moved through an arch into the kitchen. "Come on in, then," she called.

Sitting across from her at the table, glasses of orange soda between them, he was further struck by the disorganized quality of the move. The number of boxes seemed sadly inadequate to the task, and it seemed like things were being packed piecemeal: some dishes were wrapped in newspaper and stowed, while others were still stacked in cupboards or piled, dirty, in the sink; drawers hung open, partially disemboweled.

Before Jeremy could open his mouth, Rebecca said, "They's foreclosing on us. We got to be out by the weekend."

For a moment he was speechless. ". . . I . . . Jesus, Becca."

She sat there and watched him. He could think of nothing to say, so he just said, "I had no idea."

"Well, Dennis ain't been paid for a long time before he was killed, and he sure as shit hadn't been paid since then, so I guess anybody ought to of seen this comin."

He felt like he'd been punched in the gut. He didn't know if she'd meant it as an accusation, but it felt like one. It didn't help that it was true. He looked at the orange soda in the glass, a weird dash of cheerful color in all this gloom. He couldn't take his eyes off it. "What are you gonna do?"

"Well," she said, staring at her fingers as they twined around each other, "I don't really know, Jeremy. My mama lives out by Hickory, but that's a ways away, and she don't have enough room in her house for all of us. Dennis ain't spoke with his family in years. These boys don't even *know* their grandparents on his side."

He nodded. In the other room, the boys were quiet, no doubt listening in.

"I need some money, Jeremy. I mean I need it real bad. We got to be out of here in four days and we don't have no where to go." She looked up at the clock on the wall, a big round one with Roman numerals, a bright basket of fruit painted in the center. "I'm gonna lose all my things," she said. She wiped at the corner of an eye with the inside of her wrist.

Jeremy felt the twist in his gut, like his insides were being spooled on a wheel. He had to close his eyes and ride it out.

He'd sat at this table many times while Rebecca cooked for Dennis and for him; he'd been sitting here sharing a six-pack with Dennis when the call came from the hospital that their youngest had come early. "Oh, Becca," he said.

"I just need a little so we can stay someplace for a few weeks. You know, just until we can figure something out."

"Becca, I don't have it. I just don't have it. I'm so sorry."

"Jeremy, we got no where to go!"

"I don't have anything. I got collection agencies so far up my ass . . . Tara and I put the house up, Becca. The bank's threatening us, too. We can't stay where we are. We're borrowing just to keep our heads above water."

"*I can fucking sue you!*" she screamed, slapping her hand on the table so hard that the glasses toppled over and spilled orange soda all over the floor. "*You owe us! You never paid Dennis, and you owe us! I called a lawyer and he said I can sue your ass for every fucking cent you got!*"

The silence afterward was profound, broken only by the pattering of the soda trickling onto the linoleum floor.

The outburst broke a dam inside her; her face crumpled, and tears spilled over. She put a hand over her face and her body jerked silently. Jeremy looked toward the living room and saw one of the boys, his blonde hair buzzed down to his scalp, staring into the kitchen in shock.

"It's okay, Tyler," he said. "It's okay, buddy."

The boy appeared not to hear him. He watched his mother until she pulled her hand from her face and seemed to suck it all back into herself; without looking to the doorway, she fluttered a hand in the boy's direction. "It's fine, Tyler," she said. "Go help your brothers." The boy retreated.

Jeremy reached across the table and clasped her hands in his own. "Becca," he said, "you and the boys are like family to me. If I could give you some money, I would. I swear to God I would. And you're right, I do owe it to you. Dennis didn't get paid towards the end. Nobody did. So if you feel like you gotta sue me, then do it. Do what you have to do. I don't blame you. I really don't."

She looked at him, tears beading in her eyes, and said nothing.

"Shit, if suing me might keep you in your house a little while longer—if it'll keep the bank away, or something—then you should do it. I want you to do it."

Rebecca shook her head. "It won't. It's too late for that now." She rested her head on her arm, her hands still clasped in Jeremy's. "I ain't gonna sue you, Jer. It ain't your fault."

She pulled her hands free and got up. She grabbed a roll of paper towels and tore off a great handful, setting to work on the spill. "Look at this damn mess," she said.

He watched her for a moment. "I have liens on those houses we built," he said. "They can't sell them until they pay us first. The minute they do, you'll get your money."

"They won't ever finish those houses, Jer. Ain't nobody gonna want to buy them. Not after what happened."

He stayed quiet, because he knew she was right. He had privately given up on seeing that money long ago.

"A man from the bank come by last week and put that notice on the door. He had a sheriff with him. Can you believe that? A sheriff come to my house. Parked right in my driveway, for everybody to see." She paused in her work. "He was so rude," she said, her voice quiet and dismayed. "The both of them were. He told me I had to get out of my own house. My boys were standing right by me, and they just bust out crying. He didn't give a damn. Treated me like I was dirt. Might as well of called me white trash to my face."

"I'm so sorry, Becca."

"And he was such a *little* man," she said, still astonished at the memory of it. "I kept thinking how if Dennis was here that man would of *never* talked to me like that. He wouldn't of *dared!*"

Jeremy stared at his hands. Large hands, built for hard work. Useless now. Rebecca sat on the floor, fighting back tears. She gave up on the orange soda, seeming to sense the futility of it.


It was a week before Christmas, and Tara was talking to him from inside the shower. The door was open and he could see her pale shape behind the curtain, but he couldn't make out what she was saying. He sat on the bed in his underwear, his clothes for the evening laid out beside him. It was the same suit he'd worn to the funerals, and he dreaded putting it on again.

Outside the short wintertime afternoon was giving way to evening. The Christmas lights strung along the eaves and wound into the bushes still had to be turned on. The neighbors across the street had already lit theirs; the colored lights looked like glowing candy, turning their home into a gingerbread house from a fairy tale. The full moon was resplendent

Jeremy supposed that a Christmas party full of elementary school professionals might be the worst place in the world. He would drift among them helplessly, like a grizzly bear in a roomful of children, expected not to eat anyone.

He heard the squeak of the shower faucet and suddenly his wife's voice carried to him. "—time it takes to get there," she said.

"What?"

She slid the curtain open and pulled a towel from the shelf. "Have you been listening to me?"

"I couldn't hear you over the water."

She went to work on her hair. "I've just had a very lively conversation with myself, then."

"Sorry."

"Are *you* going to get dressed?" she said.

He loved to watch her like this, when she was naked but not trying to be sexy, when she was just going about the minor business of being a human being. Unself-conscious and miraculous.

"Are you?" he said.

"Very funny. You were in that same position when I started my shower. What's up?"

"I don't want to go."

She turned the towel into a blue turban and wrapped another around her body. She crossed the room and sat beside him, leaving wet footprints in the carpet, her shoulders and her face still glistening with beaded water.

"You'll catch cold," he said.

"What are you worried about?"

"I'm obese. I'm a fricking spectacle. I'm not fit to be seen in public."

"You're my handsome man."

"Stop it."

"Jeremy," she said, "you can't turn into a shut-in. You have to get out. It's been six months, and you've totally disengaged from the world. These people are safe, okay? They're not going to judge you. They're my friends, and I want them to be your friends, too."

"They're going to look at me and think, that's the guy that left his friends on a mountain to die."

"You're alive," Tara said, sharply, and turned his head so he had to look at her. "You're alive because you left. I still have a husband because you left. So in the end I don't give a shit what people think." She paused, took a steady breath, and let him go. "And not everyone's thinking bad things about you. Sometimes you have to take people at face value, Jeremy. Sometimes people really are what they say they are."

He nodded, chastened. He knew she was right. He'd been hiding in this house for months. It had to stop.

She touched his cheek and smiled at him. "Okay?"

"Yeah. Okay."

She got up and headed back to the bathroom, and he fell back on the bed. "Okay," he said.

"Besides," she called back happily, "don't forget about Tim! Someone has to keep the beast at bay!"

A sudden, coursing heat pulsed through him. He had forgotten Tim. "Oh yeah," he said, sitting up. He watched her dress, her body incandescent with water and light, and felt something like hope move inside him.


The house was bigger than Jeremy had been expecting. It was in an upscale subdivision, where all the houses had at least two stories and a basement. The front porch shed light like a fallen star, and colored Christmas bulbs festooned the neighborhood. "Jesus," he said, turning into the parking lot already full of cars. "Donny lives *here?*"

Donny Winn was the vice-principal of the school: a rotund, pink-faced man who sweated a lot and always seemed on the brink of a nervous breakdown. Jeremy had only met him once or twice, but the man made an impression like a damp cloth.

"His wife's a physical therapist," Tara said. "She works with the Carolina Panthers or something. Trust me, she's the money."

The house was packed. Jeremy didn't recognize anybody. A table in the dining room had been pushed against a wall and its wings extended, turning it into a buffet table loaded with an assortment of holiday dishes and confections. Bowls of spiked eggnog anchored each end of the table. Donny leaned against a wall nearby, alone but smiling. His wife worked the crowd like a politician, steering newly-arrived guests toward the table and bludgeoning them with goodwill.

Christmas lights were strung throughout the house, and mistletoe hung in every doorway. Andy Williams crooned from speakers hidden by the throng.

Jeremy wended his way through the mill of people behind Tara, who guided him to the table. Within moments they were armed with booze and ready for action. Jeremy spoke into Tara's ear. "Where's Tim?"

She craned her neck and looked around, then shook her head. "I can't see him. Don't worry. He'll find us!"

"You mean he'll find *you*," he said.

She smiled and squeezed his hand.

He measured time in drinks, and then he lost track of it. The lights and the sounds were beginning to blur into a candy-hued miasma that threatened to drown him. He'd become stationary in the middle of the living room, people and conversations revolving around him like the spokes of some demented Ferris wheel. Tara was beside him, nearly doubled over in laughter, one hand gripping his upper arm in a vise as she talked to a gaunt, heavily made-up woman whose eyes seemed to reflect light like sheets of ice.

"He's evil!" The woman had to shout to be heard. "His parents should have strangled him at birth!"

"Jesus," Jeremy said, trying to remember what they were talking about.

"Oh my God, Jeremy, you don't know this kid," Tara said. "He's got like—this *look*. I'm serious! Totally dead."

The woman nodded eagerly. "And the other day? I was looking through their daily journals? I found a picture of a severed head."

"What? No way!"

"The neck was even drawn with jagged red lines, to show it was definitely cut off. To make sure I knew it!"

"Somebody should do something," Jeremy said. "We're gonna be reading about this little monster someday."

Tara shook her head. "Nobody wants to know anymore. 'Boys will be boys,' right?"

The woman arched an eyebrow. "People are just fooled by the packaging," she said. "Kids shouldn't be drawing severed heads!"

Tara laughed. "But it's okay for grown-ups to?"

"Nobody should draw them," the woman said gravely.

"Excuse me," Jeremy said, and moved away from them both. He felt Tara's hand on his arm, but he kept going. The conversation had rattled him.

Severed heads. What the fuck!

He slid clumsily through the crowd, using his weight to help along the people who were slow in getting out of his way. He found himself edging past the hostess, who smiled at him and said "Merry Christmas," her eyes sliding away from him before the words were even out of her mouth. He was briefly overwhelmed by a spike of outrage at her blithe manner—at the whole apparatus of entitlement and assumption this party suddenly represented to him, with its abundance and its unapologetic stink of money. "I'm Jewish," he said, and felt a happy thrill when she whipped her head around as he pressed further into the crowd.

He stationed himself by the fireplace, which was, at the moment, free of people. He set his drink on the mantel and turned his back to the crowd, looking instead at the carefully arranged manger scene on display there. The ceramic pieces were old and chipped; it had clearly been in the family for a long time. He looked past the wise men and the shepherds crouched in reverent awe, and saw the baby Jesus at the focal point, his little face rosy pink, his mouth a gaping oval, one eye chipped away. Jeremy's flesh rippled and he turned away.

And then he saw Tim approaching through the crowd. Tim was a slight man, with thinning hair and a pair of silver-rimmed glasses. Jeremy decided he looked like a cartoonist's impression of an intellectual. He stared at him as he approached.

This was what he had come for. He felt the blood start to move in his body, slowly, like a river breaking through ice floes. He felt some measure of himself again. It was just as intoxicating as the liquor.

Tim held out his hand, still closing the distance, and Jeremy took it. "Hey. Jeremy, right? Tara's husband?"

"Yeah. I'm sorry, you are?"

"Oh I'm Tim Duckett, we met last year, at that teachers' union thing?"

"Oh yeah. Tim, hey."

"I just saw you over here by yourself and I thought, that guy is frickin lost. You know? Totally out of his element."

Jeremy bristled. "I think you made a mistake."

"Really? I mean, look at these people." He shifted to stand beside Jeremy so they could look out over the crowd together. "Come on. *Tea*chers? This is hell for *me!* I can only imagine how you must feel."

"I feel just fine."

Tim touched his glass to Jeremy's. "Well here's to you then. I feel like I'm about to fucking choke." He took a deep drink. "I mean, look at that guy over there. The fat one?" Jeremy flushed but held his tongue. These people didn't think. "That's Shane Mueller," Tim continued. "Laughing like he's high or something. He can afford to laugh because he's got the right friends, you know what I mean? Goddamn arrogant prick. Not like her."

He gestured at the woman Jeremy had been talking to just a few moments ago. Where was Tara?

"Word is she's not coming back next year. She won't be the only one, either. Everybody here's scared shitless. The fucking legislature's throwing us to the wolves. Who cares about education, right? Not when there's dollars at stake." He took a drink. "*English?* Are you kidding me?"

Tim sidled up next to him, so that their arms brushed. Jeremy gave a small push with his elbow and Tim surrendered some ground, seeming not to notice.

"I always kind of envied you, you know?" he was saying.

". . . what?"

"Oh yeah. Probably freaks you out, right? This guy you barely even know? But Tara talks about you in the lounge sometimes, and it got to where I felt like I kind of knew you a little bit."

"So you like to talk to Tara, huh?"

"Oh yeah man, she's a great girl. Great girl. But what you do is real work. You hang out with grown men and build things. With your *hands.*" He held out his own hands, as though to illustrate the concept. "I hang out with kids, man." He gestured at the crowd. "A bunch of goddamn kids."

Jeremy took a drink. He peered into his glass. The ice had almost completely melted, leaving a murky, diluted puddle at the bottom. "Things change," he said.

Tim gave him a fierce, sympathetic look. "Yeah, you've been through some shit, haven't you?"

Jeremy looked at him, dimly amazed, feeling suddenly defensive. This guy had no boundaries. "What?"

"Come on, man, we all know. It's not like it's a secret, right? That fucking wolf?"

"You don't know shit."

"Now that's not fair. If you don't want to talk about it, okay, I get that. But we were all here for Tara when it happened. She's got a lot of friends here. It's not like we're totally uninvested."

Jeremy turned on him, a sudden wild heat burning his skin from the inside. He pressed his body against Tim's and backed him against the fireplace. Tim nearly tripped on the hearth and grabbed the mantel to keep his balance. "I said you don't know *shit.*"

Tim's face was stretched in surprise. "Holy shit, Jeremy, are you gonna hit me?"

Jeremy felt a hand on his shoulder, and he heard his wife's voice. "What's going on here?"

He backed off, letting her pull him away, and allowing Tim to regain his balance. Tim stared at the two of them, looking more bemused now than worried or affronted.

Tara laced her hand into her husband's. "Do you boys need a time-out?"

Tim made a placating gesture. "No, no, we're just talking about—"

"Tim's just running his mouth," Jeremy said. "He needs to learn to shut it."

Tara squeezed his hand and leaned against him. He could feel the tension in her body. "Why don't we get some fresh air?" she said.

"What?"

"Come on. I want to see the lights outside."

"Don't you try to placate me. What's the matter with you?"

Tim said, "Whoa, whoa, let's all calm down a little bit."

"Why don't you shut the fuck up."

The sound of the party continued unabated, but Jeremy could sense a shift in the atmosphere around him. He didn't have to turn around to know that he was beginning to draw attention.

"Jeremy!" Tara's voice was sharp. "What the hell has gotten into you?"

Tim touched her arm. "It's my fault. I brought up the wolf thing."

Jeremy grabbed his wrist. "If you touch my wife one more time I'll break your goddamn arm." His mind flooded with images of operatic violence, of Tim's guts garlanding all the expensive furniture like Christmas bunting. He rode the crest of this wave with radiant joy.

Astonishingly, Tim grinned at him. "What the fuck, man?"

Jeremy watched Tim's lips pull back, saw the display of teeth, and surrendered himself to instinct. It was like dropping a chain; the freedom and the relief that coursed through his body was almost religious in its impact. Jeremy hit him in the mouth as hard as he could. Something sharp and jagged tore his knuckles. Tim flailed backwards, tripping on the hearth again but this time falling hard. His head knocked the mantel on the way down, leaving a bloody postage stamp on the white paint. Manger pieces toppled over the side and bounced off him.

Someone behind him shrieked. Voices rose in a chorus, but it was all just background noise. Jeremy leaned over and hit him again and again, until several hands grabbed him from behind and heaved him backward, momentarily lifting him off his feet. He was grappled by a cluster of men, his arms twisted behind him and immobilized. The whole mass of them lurched about like some demented monster, as Jeremy tried to break free.

The room had gone quiet. "Silver Bells" went on for another few seconds until someone rushed to the stereo and switched it off. All he could hear was his own heavy breathing.

He resumed a measure of control over himself, though his blood still galloped through his head and his muscles still jerked with energy. "Okay," he said. "Okay."

He found himself at the center of the crowd, most of them standing well back and staring agape. Someone was crouched beside Tim, who was sitting on the hearth, his face pale; his hands cupped beneath his bloody mouth. One eye was already swelling shut.

Tara stood to one side, her face red with anger, or humiliation, or both. She marched forward and grabbed him forcibly by the bicep, and yanked him behind her. The men holding him let him go.

"Should we call the police?" someone said.

"Oh *fuck you!*" Tara shouted.

She propelled him through the front door and out into the cold air. She did not release him until they arrived at the truck. The night arced over them both, and the world was bespangled with Christmas-colored constellations. Tara sagged against the truck's door, hiding her face against the window. He stood silently, trying to grasp for some feeling here, for some appropriate mode of behavior. Now that the adrenaline was fading, it was starting to dawn on him how bad this was.

Tara stood up straight and said, without looking at him, "I have to go back inside for a minute. Wait here."

"Do you want me to go with you?"

"Just wait here."

He did. She went up to the front door and rang the bell, and after a moment she was let inside. He stood there and let the cold work its way through his body, banking the last warm embers of the alcohol. After a while he got behind the wheel of the truck and waited. Soon, the front door opened again, and she came out. She walked briskly to the truck, her breath trailing behind her, and opened his door. "Move over," she said. "I'm driving."

He didn't protest. Moments later she started the engine and pulled onto the road. She drive them slowly out of the neighborhood, until the last big house receded into the darkness behind them, like a glittering piece of jewelry dropped into the ocean. She steered them onto the highway, and they eased onto the long stretch home.

"He's not going to call the police," she said at last. "Small miracle."

He nodded. "I thought you wanted me to confront him," he said, and regretted it immediately.

She didn't respond. He stole a glance at her: her face was unreadable. She drew in a deep breath. "Did you tell Mrs. Winn that we're Jewish?"

". . . yeah."

"Why? Why would you do that?"

He just shook his head and stared out the window. Lights streaked by, far away.

Tara sobbed once, both hands still clutching the steering wheel. Her face was twisted in misery. "You have to get a hold of yourself," she said. "I don't know what's happening to you. I don't know what to do."

He leaned his head back and closed his eyes. He felt his guts turn to stone. He knew he had to say something, he had to try to explain himself here, or someday she would leave. Maybe someday soon. But the fear was too tight; it wouldn't let him speak. It would barely let him breathe.


When they get home Jeremy cannot bear the strained silence. After an hour of it he escapes in the truck, making a trip to the attic before he leaves. Now he's speeding down a winding two-lane blacktop, going so fast he can't stay in his lane. If anyone else appears on this road, everybody's fucked. He makes a fast right when he comes to the turn-in for Wild Acre, the truck hitting the bumps in the road too hard and smashing its undercarriage into the dirt. He pushes it up the hill, the untended dirt road overgrown with weeds. The truck judders around a bend, something groaning under the hood. The wheel slips out of his hands and the truck slides into a ditch, coming to a crunching halt and slamming Jeremy's face into the steering wheel.

The headlights peer crookedly into the dust-choked air, illuminating the house frames, which look like huge, drifting ghosts behind curtains of raised dirt and clay. He leans back in his seat, gingerly touching his nose, and his vision goes watery. The full moon leaks silver blood into the sky. Something inside him buckles, and acid fills his mouth. He puts a hand over it, squeezes his eyes shut, and thinks, Don't you do it, don't you fucking do it.

He doesn't do it. He swallows it back, burning his throat.

He slams his elbow into the door several times. Then he rests his head on the steering wheel and sobs. These are huge, body-breaking sobs, the kind that leave him gasping for breath, the kind he hasn't suffered since he was a little kid. They frighten him a little. He is not meant to sound like this.

After a few moments he stops, lifts his head, and stares at the closest house frame, bone-colored in the moonlight. The floor is covered in dark stains. The forest is surging behind it. In a scramble of terror he wrenches the rifle from its rack, opens the door and jumps into the road.

The gun is slippery in his hands. He strides into the house frame and raises the gun to his chin, aiming it into the dark forest, staring down the sight. The world and its sounds retreat into a single point of stillness. He watches, and waits.

"Come on!" he screams. "Come on! *Come on!*"

But nothing comes.

# S.S.

*In the morning before going to work, Nick* found his mother and gave her a kiss. He used the flashlight to locate her, careful as always to keep the beam from touching her. This time she was in the kitchen, her wheelchair backed into a small alcove between the refrigerator and the oven. She seemed only barely conscious when he reached her, which was not unusual; her head bobbed gently when his lips touched her cheek, as though nodding in recognition. When he backed away from her he almost tripped over a plate she had left lying on the floor. A quick scan with the flashlight revealed the bright red splash of blood on the china, a glaring arc of beauty like a detail from a Pollock canvas. Nick retrieved the plate and placed it in the sink. He went back to his mother and made sure the blanket was secure around her legs, and that she was warm.

The kiss was an act of duty and of love; if there was a difference between them, Nick did not recognize it.

Miss Josephine's was a little Cajun restaurant half a block off the distal end of Bourbon Street, in what Nick had always thought of as the Fag District. It was far enough from the main drag that the owner claimed to be unable to afford an air conditioner in the kitchen. So the staff opened the delivery door, admitting the warm, viscous subtropical air, laced with the perfume of rotting garbage coming from the trash bags stacked along the curb every afternoon. The kitchen was tiny and cramped, even with only the three employees: Nick, who labored over the steamy exhalations of the power washer; and the two black line cooks, Tyrone and Big Jake. When business was slow—which was nearly always—and there were few dishes to wash, the owner justified Nick's hours by having him prep food for the night shift and sometimes for the following day. This work consisted of peeling potatoes, cleaning spinach, de-veining shrimp, and skinning and cutting long, phallic ropes of andouille sausage. In this way, Nick was paid as a dishwasher but employed as a prep cook. Nick reasoned to himself that the owner, being a Jew, was only acting according to his nature, which made it easier for him to accept. Furthermore, the circumstances at home did not allow him the luxury of quitting.

The owner was an overweight, meticulously tidy man named Barry Bright—a failed car salesman from Idaho, and about as far from an actual Cajun as it was possible to get. When he walked through the kitchen it was with as much reluctance and mincing care as a man crossing a grassy median carpeted with dog turds. He stepped gingerly around the extended arms of simmering pots and refused to walk over the rubber mats behind the line, which were often caked with squashed gobs of meat and vegetable. The heat made him sweat, and because he was a large man he did so with vigorous industry, ruining his temper and his shirts. He hated being in the kitchen; when he had to address the kitchen staff he preferred to do it in the dining area, where he couldn't afford *not* to run an air conditioner. So when the kitchen door swung open and he stepped back there, everyone stopped what they were doing to watch. He pointed a finger at Nick and jerked his head back the way he had come. "Nick! What I tell you about phone calls at work!"

Nick set down the knife he was using to chop garlic and made a helpless gesture. "I didn't call no one, Mr. Bright."

"Somebody called *you*. Come out here and get it. She says it's important." He cast a disparaging glance around the kitchen. "You boys better get this pigsty cleaned up before the night shift comes in." He looked at Big Jake, a huge man of indeterminate age and immeasurable girth. "You got it under control in here, Jake?"

"Always do, Mr. Bright."

Bright nodded curtly and retreated into the dining area. Nick followed him out, taking off his hat and wiping a rag over his closely shaven head.

When he picked up the phone, he found Trixie waiting on the other end of it.

"You gotta do something, Nick," she said, without preamble.

"Hey," he said. "I thought you were mad at me."

"Stupid. Why would I be mad at you?"

"I don't know. 'Cause I ran out of there, I guess." It had been nearly a week since the meeting at Derrick's apartment, and he hadn't heard from her at all in that time. He'd been sure she had cut him loose.

She was silent a moment, which let him know he wasn't absolved. "Well, you didn't exactly help yourself out," she said. "What happened there, anyway?"

"I don't know," he muttered, leaning against the counter. His chef's coat released little scent-clouds of garlic and onion whenever he moved. He saw Mr. Bright watching him from across the restaurant. "Fuck them. Derrick's an asshole; he doesn't want me in the group anyway."

"Yes he does, but he's not gonna just give you a free pass. To him you're just some punk kid. My word gets you in the door, but after that it's on you."

"Yeah, well, I don't know if I want to mess with it. They hate me anyway. They think I'm a pussy."

"Well are you?"

The question caught him off guard, and it hurt. "What? What's that supposed to mean?"

"I don't know, Nickie. You seem to be ready to give it all up."

"Give what up? I'm not in their fucking group."

"No, but I am."

After a moment he said, "So it's like that." Something was opening up in his chest, some painful bloom, and when he drew in a breath it caught fire like a smoldering coal. He put his hand over his eyes and felt his throat constrict.

"This is who I am, Nickie. It's part of the package."

Bright called something from across the room and pointed at his watch. Nick turned his back to him. "I don't know if I can do it, Trix," he said. "I don't know if I care enough. Does that make me a traitor? Does that make me a bad guy?"

She seemed honestly to consider it. Finally she said, "Not to the race, maybe. But to me. Do you care about me, Nickie?"

"Yeah," he said; then, more forcefully: "Yes. You're the only thing I care about."

"Let me come over tonight."

"Oh, Trix, I don't think so."

"Please. You never let me see where you live."

Nick watched his boss come closer, standing in the middle of the dining area and staring at him openly. "It's so fucked up over there. I mean, you just don't know."

"I thought you said you cared about me." When he didn't respond, she said, "We're at a major turning point in our relationship, Nickie. You gotta let me come over. Otherwise I don't know what to think."

He considered a moment. "Fine," he said. "Come over. But my mom is crazy."

"I know, you told me."

"No, I mean really fucking crazy. So, whatever. Come over if you want. But you're not gonna want to stay." He nodded at Mr. Bright and said, "Look, I gotta go. Emperor Zog is looking at me like I stole a nickel."

"I'll see you tonight," she said, and hung up the phone.

When he walked back into the kitchen, Big Jake chucked him on the arm. "Boss Man must like you," he said.

"Funny, it don't seem that way to me."

"Trust me. My wife call me, she got to be havin a baby before he even think about comin back here."

Tyrone shook his head and made a noise of disbelief. "One thing you don't need is no more babies," he said.

Big Jake laughed. "I know you right!"

"What you got, big man, roun' forty?"

The two men laughed and began to banter, and just like that Nick passed from their attention, like an amusing notion considered and discarded. He picked up his chef's knife and went back to work on the garlic. "Maybe you stop havin so many kids, you won't have to work three jobs," he said sullenly.

They stopped talking.

"What you say?" Tyrone said, squinting curiously at him, as though trying to figure out what variety of lunatic he was faced with.

Tyrone was only a few years older than Nick; he had grown up in the St. Thomas project before the city tore it down and kicked everybody out. He and Nick worked all right together as long as they didn't talk directly to each other.

Nick stopped what he was doing and looked at him. "I'm just saying use some fucking common sense. That's why my paycheck is so fucking small every week, 'cause the government's gotta take care of y'all's goddamn kids."

"Oh, *shit!*"

"This ain't even about you, T," said Nick. "Jake's the daddy. I'm talking to him. Be responsible, dude, that's all."

"What you think workin three jobs *is*, bitch?" said Tyrone.

Big Jake put a hand on Tyrone's shoulder. "This ain't the place," he said. Then he pointed one massive finger at Nick and said, "You better settle down, man. Your young ass got no idea what you even talking about."

Nick nodded and returned his attention to the garlic. "It's cool, Jake."

After that, the kitchen was mostly quiet until two-thirty, when Nick's shift ended. He punched his timecard and signed it; when he turned to leave he found himself staring at Tyrone, who'd come up behind him and left him no room to edge around. Nick took a reflexive step backward and was brought up short by the time clock. He'd thought that after the incident at Derrick's place he would be anxious for a chance to redeem himself, but now that he was faced with a real confrontation, he felt his body quail. He became powerfully aware of how much larger Tyrone was than himself, and how many awful things could happen to a person in a kitchen.

But he pressed up to Tyrone until their chests were touching and their faces were only inches apart, in a kind of grotesque intimacy. "What you wanna do?" he said.

"Nazi motherfucker," Tyrone said. "You get in my face sometime. See how it go for you then."

"What you wanna do, T?"

"Like I said. Try it and see."

Big Jake slammed a pan down behind them, making Nick jump. "Goddammit, get your silly ass outta here! T, get back on the line! We got tickets comin in."

"I'm going, I'm going," said Nick, and he slid around Tyrone and headed out into the warm October afternoon, where he kept walking until he was out of sight of the restaurant and then leaned against the painted brick of a 24-hour bar, breathing deeply, while his heart threw out flaring arcs of rage and frustration like an effulgent red star.

Nick's mother used to say that they'd lost his father to the horses.

Throughout his childhood, Nick thought that meant that he'd been killed by them: trampled beneath a galloping herd, or thrown from the back of a bronco; when he was younger still, he imagined that they'd devoured him, dipping their great regal heads into the open bowl of his body, lifting them out again trailing bright ropes and jellies. At night, when the closet door in his bedroom swung silently open, the boogeyman wore an equine face, and the sound that spilled from its mouth was the dolorous melody of his mother's sobs. Even now that he knew better, knew that his father had fled in part because of gambling debts incurred at the track, horses retained their sinister aspect.

His mother's frequent struggles with depression apparently taxed his father beyond endurance, and what comfort he couldn't find at home he made for himself at the Fair Grounds. He left them when Nick was four years old; he'd burned through their life savings, and apparently decided that there was nothing else worth coming home to. He existed from then on as a monthly child-support check, which supplemented his mother's income as a receptionist in a dentist's office.

But even that changed a few months ago, when the high school guidance counselor took him aside and informed him that his mother had been in a serious car accident. She was at the hospital, and it was not known if she would survive. He took Nick back to his office, and they waited there for well over an hour, Nick sipping a lukewarm carton of chocolate milk from the cafeteria, the counselor looking at him with naked, cloying concern, his whole body freighted with the sympathy of the uninvolved.

She survived, of course: paralyzed from the waist down; both feet removed; with a grotesque head wound that became a scar so large that her left eye seemed pulled out of true, giving her a wild, glaring aspect even while she slept. She commenced a free fall into depression, unable to work and neglecting the bills until the utilities were cut off and mortgage payments went delinquent. Finally he understood that the medical bills far outweighed her negligible insurance, and that they were in dire financial straits. She developed an antipathy to sunlight, covering the windows with heavy curtains and protesting angrily even when he lit too many candles at night. Darkness pooled in the house and grew stagnant; shortly afterward, his mother's affliction manifested into its current gruesome incarnation. It was his duty to assist her, and to clean the blood off the plates when she was finished.

His father's monthly checks still arrived, but the man who wrote them maintained an absolute radio silence that swallowed all hope of rescue.

It was around this time that he found Trixie—or rather, that Trixie decided to retrieve him from the scrap heap of social inconsequence, for reasons which were still mysterious to him. She provided him with an excuse to spend more time away from the house, which was almost as good as spending time with her. It was a precarious but practicable existence, until it became clear that his father's checks would not be enough to sustain it. He would have to get a job.

So three weeks ago he waited by his high school's front gate for the final class to let out. He spotted Trixie coming down the steps and remained there until she strolled up to him. Her red checkered skirt and white blouse seemed absurd in the context of her closely shorn hair, the enticing hint of a tattoo looping down below her right sleeve, and the openly confrontational stance she maintained with the school and just about everybody in it. She was a year older than he was, but to him it seemed as though she was from another, more sophisticated country, where people were cool and didn't take any shit, and where they believed in themselves absolutely. That she had recently seen fit to spend time with him was a stroke of luck that very nearly compensated for his mother's dismal condition.

"What's up, gorgeous?" she said, falling in step with him as he turned away from the school. She started unbuttoning her shirt, revealing the white tank top she wore underneath. He could see her black bra through it, and again he wondered at his fortune. "Playing hooky today?"

"No," he said. They walked a few steps, and he added, "I'm quitting school."

"Holy shit, no way! Are you serious?" She looked at him with a mixture of alarm and delight.

"Yeah. Mom made me."

This was apparently too much. She threw out her arms and pinwheeled along the sidewalk, yelling, "Oh my God, no way! You have the coolest fucking mom!"

Nick just shook his head and watched her dance off her gleeful burst of energy. "She had to quit her job, so I gotta work. It's not like I get to do what I want."

"Yeah, but Nickie! Oh my God, I wish I had your mom." She considered a moment. "Hey, that would make you my brother, wouldn't it? Mmm, kinky."

Nick blushed and turned his face to hide it. She still hadn't let him so much as touch her breasts, yet she taunted him flagrantly with these constant sexual references. Sometimes he wondered if she was using him as a kind of science project, in which she was trying to determine just how much provocation a teenage boy could endure before his hair caught fire.

"Where are you gonna work?"

"I don't know, somewhere in the Quarter, I guess. I can always get a job washing dishes or something."

She looked stunned. "That's nigger's work, Nickie!"

"Well, what the fuck, Trix, I don't have any skills. I gotta make money somehow."

She nodded absently and kept whatever she was thinking to herself. As per routine, they bussed down to the French Quarter, where they played video games at the arcade until it started to get dark. For a time he submerged himself in the surf of the arcade's fuzzy explosions and kaleidoscopic light show, content with the warm proximity of this strange beautiful girl and the narcotic effect of the video games, with their offerings of bright cartoon villains and violent catharsis.

"You know those meetings I go to every Thursday?" said Trixie.

Of course he did. They meant he couldn't hang out with her much on Thursdays; the two of them had to forego the Quarter altogether and hang out in one of those insufferable Uptown coffee shops, which he hated almost as much as he hated going to school. He tried not to speculate about what she did at those meetings, but because she told him nothing, even telling him to mind his own business on the one occasion he did ask, they had become cauldrons of evil possibility: maybe she got drunk with older, more sophisticated boys, or posed nude for some college art class.

"Yeah," he said. "I always figured it was church or something."

"Stupid. Can you see me in a church?" She thought about it, and he watched her face settle into a more serious cast. "Although maybe that's not too far off. It *is* people who believe in something more important than themselves. So I guess it's like a church. Or a family."

He nodded. "I see." He wondered if he was about to get dumped. He felt suddenly light, as though he had no real substance, as though if she said the words he was waiting to hear he would just dissolve into the atmosphere, like a sigh.

"You seem like you could use a family," she said.

He looked at her. Time snagged around her words, where it fluttered, waiting to be set free again.

"I been telling them about you. They want to meet you."

It came loose and drifted free, a red silk banner twisting into a blue sky.


"And now he's all, he's blubbering like a little baby, he's got snot coming out of his nose. 'Oh please don't kill me, please don't kill me,

I'll suck your dick, please don't kill me!'" Derrick's voice goes high in a falsetto imitation. "And dude, what did you do, Matt? What did you fuckin do?"

Matt shrugged. "I took my dick out."

"He did! Matt here whips it out and says well go on then! Get to it!" Derrick paused while the others laughed. He was telling this story to all four guys sitting on stools at the bar in this little dive tavern on the Westbank, across the bridge from downtown New Orleans. The four guys Nick was with were all heavily muscled, with shaved heads and elaborate tattoos. Derrick was the biggest of them; he wore a thin wifebeater, and Nick couldn't help but stare enviously at all his muscles, at his arms and back covered with swastikas, bloody-fanged skulls, and, over his heart, crossed hammers against the backdrop of a Confederate flag. He looked to Nick like the apotheosis of man, some rarefied ideal of physical and mental presence. It was a little past seven and the bar was not crowded. Nick felt the atmosphere change when they walked in, felt the gravity of their presence draw every eyeball in the building. When they settled in and ordered beers, the fat man behind the bar who brought the drinks to them wouldn't even look them in the eye. Nick, clearly underage, didn't warrant a glance.

Matt, a little fireplug of a kid, was on the other side of Derrick. "Tell him the rest of the story before he starts thinking I'm some kinda fag."

"So this little queer crawls over to Matt and starts to reach out for his dick, still bawling, and Matt fucking balls up his fist and fucking drills him in the head! *Crack!* Motherfucker drops like he's dead."

"I thought he was," Matt said, taking a sip from his bottle. "I was like, goddamn, he really *is* a pussy."

"He wasn't dead, though. He was still crawling around, making this weird little sound. We kicked him around a little bit, and then I fucking curb-stomped him to make my point."

"Shit," Matt said. "You did that boy a favor. He probably sucks *good* dick now." While the others laughed and shook their heads, Derrick said, "You believe that story, Nick?"

"Sure. I guess."

"Oh, he guesses. My man here guesses."

The bar had gathered all the residual heat of the afternoon and hoarded it with a miser's resolve. A ceiling fan whickered pointlessly, stirring the thick air like a spoon in a honeypot. Trixie was back at Derrick's apartment with the other girls, hanging out doing whatever until the boys were done talking business. They would give them time to talk and then they'd show up later. Women were rarely welcomed into meetings such as this. The point of the meeting, Trixie had told him, would be to judge his worth as a recruit to the Confederate Hammers, the regional chapter of the white nationalist movement called the Hammerskin Nation.

"Do you even get that point of that story, Nick? That dude was a junkie. He was sucking cock for drugs. Now you know, whatever, the world's full of human cockroaches, I can't worry about all of that shit or I'll go crazy, right? But it was in my neighborhood. He's walking up and down the goddamn street, cracked out of his mind, talking all this shit a mile a minute so it made you crazy just to hear it. In *this goddamn neighborhood*. We got kids that live here, you know what I mean? Got so I just couldn't stand for it anymore."

He touched his fingers to a swastika on his chest. "You see this here? That's what it means. That's why we wear it on our skin. All that German secret police shit, forget all that. That was just one manifestation. We're the new manifestation." He tapped the symbol. "White family. White brotherhood. Now, sometimes you gotta do ugly things for the family's sake. Just like me and Matt had to do. And you know what? Niggers and fags might not be the brightest creatures on this earth, but they can take a message if you deliver it right. I ain't seen that boy back here since."

The other boys nodded. "Damn right," one said.

"Violence is the only language they understand," said Derrick. "So if you don't know it, you better learn it."

Nick nodded again. He resisted the impulse to check his watch. It seemed like Trixie and the other girls should have been here by now. He figured when the girls got back they would set aside business and just sit around and get drunk, which is what he really wanted.

"You got what it takes to earn the broken cross, Nick? Put the S.S. on your skin? You know, you got to earn it."

"I know," said Nick.

"Can you handle yourself in a fight?" The others looked him over like they couldn't really believe it. "'Cause I mean, no offense dude, but you're kind of a scrawny little fuck."

Somebody laughed.

"I can handle myself," Nick said.

"You hear that Matt? He think's he's hard."

"He don't look too hard," Matt said.

"Well. I guess we gotta ask Trix about that."

Nick flushed. Derrick leaned toward him and said, "Our girl, she knows all about hard. You think you can fill her up, little boy? She let you in there yet? She ain't a little kid. If you don't know what you're doing, you ain't gonna fool her." He grabbed his crotch, spreading his fingers to indicate he had quite a handful. "Besides, I stretched her out pretty good. I don't know if she'll be able to feel your little needle."

"Fuck you," Nick said.

"Uh-oh, here we go," said Matt. Nick glared at the floor and stood up. Derrick rose to meet him, but Nick turned toward the door."

"What?" said Derrick? "Are you going to cry? Oh my God, you are."

Nick strode toward the door. A stinging heat pressed behind his eyes.

Derrick laughed. "You sure you want to go? We got four of us, only three girls. I think Matt could use a bitch, couldn't you, Matt?"

"Fuck you dude," Matt said.

Nick opened the door and stepped outside; the evening air felt cool after the dense heat of the bar. He felt an absurd impulse to ask them to tell Trixie that he'd gone home, but crushed it. One of the boys said, "What a little bitch," and then the door shut behind him. He started the long walk to the ferry, which would carry him across the river and back into familiar territory. Streetlamps along the way shed cold trees of light. The dark sky was close and heavy.

After that, he was sure she was done with him. But this morning's phone call at the restaurant gave him new hope, and he found himself waiting for her on his front porch. He watched the evening settle over New Orleans like some great hunched buzzard, the sky deepening into the star-spiked blue of twilight. Fitful gusts of wind carried a cold undercurrent and occasionally pelted him with a few fat, isolated raindrops. Across the street, the thrashing fronds of a palm tree tossed around a bright shard of moon.

Nick and his mother lived in a shotgun house a few blocks lakeside of St. Charles Avenue, and like many other houses on their street it existed on the cusp of total dereliction. Paint peeled from its walls, and the wood was so riddled with termites that, during mating season, huge swarms of them would choke the air inside the house. Their tiny lawn seemed eager to make up for its size with outright belligerence, as though it harbored aspirations to junglehood and resented its confined circumstances. As porch lights and windows began to glow along the street, his own home grew darker by comparison, until it looked like an abandoned house, and would have likely attracted the usual doomed human ecology of abandoned houses were it not for the occasional errant stabs of light glimpsed through windows, and the mournful sounds which from time to time seemed to exhale from the building itself and spoil the air around it.

A small band of black kids made their way down the street, one of them swinging a long stick in a sweeping arc, like an explorer hacking his way through heavy foliage. They talked easily, loudly, apparently indifferent to anything in the world other than themselves and their own immediate impulses. Nick watched them come with a puzzling lack of emotion: they were just kids tonight, kids he didn't know. He tried to summon the anger he believed was justified and proper, and failed. The one with the stick whacked it against the fenders of parked cars, sending little detonations ricocheting down the street. Normally this would throw Nick into a fury, which he would nurture from the near-obscurity of his front porch; but tonight each crack of the stick vanished into a gulf inside him. As they passed in front of his house, they fell abruptly silent. They did not look at him or his house, and they held their heads back and sauntered with their customary loose-limbed bravado, but he knew the place spooked them. Sometimes that embarrassed him, other times it made him proud. Tonight he just felt defeated.

Finally they disappeared around the corner. Their voices picked up again, and soon he heard the steady, diminishing whack of the stick against metal. He waited several more minutes; the wind increased, and heavy clouds moved in to obscure the moon. Nick watched as two headlights glided around a distant corner and made their steady way to him. Trixie had finally arrived.

Before he opened the door for her, he said, "It's dark inside. They ain't cut the power back on yet."

"That's okay."

He led her inside. By now he had become accustomed to the darkness, but he remembered his first time coming home to it, and knew how Trixie must feel. It had been so overwhelming that he had actually experienced a rush of vertigo, and a brief, terrible conviction that he had been struck blind, or that perhaps he had died.

He dug a little flashlight out of his pocket and flicked it on. The grim state of their home bobbed into sight, like surfacing detritus from a sunken ship. Clothes lay in careless piles on the floor, unwashed plates and empty or nearly empty glasses—insides rimmed with coagulated syrup from soda and sweet tea—were stacked and strewn across the coffee table. Furtive shapes clicked and darted amongst them, erupting every now and then into violent skirmishes: cockroaches, which had found in his home a kind of Eden. They cloying stench of fried meat and stagnant air covered them like a shroud.

"Jesus, Nick," Trixie said.

A sound crawled toward them out of the darkness: a broken, lurching squeal, like a rat being ground beneath a boot. It was so alien, and so painful, that he half expected some nightmare creature of tall, scraping bone to amble into view, its jaw swinging loosely beneath a searching, serpentine tongue.

Nick ushered Trixie into his bedroom, located right off the living room, and gave her the flashlight. "Wait here," he said. "I got more flashlights in here you can light. I'll be right back." He shut the door on her, and turned toward the sound coming down the hallway.

It was his mother, in her grandmother's old wheelchair, looking so much older and smaller than she had before the accident. It was as though some ancient version of herself had bled back through time to confront him, dismayed and death-haunted. A blanket was bunched around her legs, which only barely registered as two thin ridges underneath. She held a votive candle in an ashtray; it was the only light she would permit herself.

"Nickie, you're home," she said. "I was worried."

"I'm okay, Mom."

"Who's here?"

"Um . . . a girl. Trixie. She's my friend."

"A girl?" She looked at the shut door of his bedroom. "Oh, my."

"I really don't wanna do this now, Mom."

"Please, Nickie. Please. I need it so bad."

"Godammit," he said. "Fine. Let's make it quick."

"Okay," she said meekly.

She led him down the hallway, the little candle casting a golden corona onto the wall as she wheeled along, so that it seemed he was following a ghost. They went into her bedroom, which was nearly unnavigable, strewn with clothes and bloody bedsheets, exuding the cloistered funk of a shut-in, even more powerful here than in the rest of the house.

"You gotta wash the sheets or something, Mom. It's rank in here."

"I'm sorry, Nickie." Her voice sounded childlike and bereft, and he felt ashamed of himself.

"Forget it. It's okay."

"I know I've been a terrible mother."

Fuck's sake, he thought, not now. He was determined to head this one off at the pass. "No, you're not. You just had a hard time."

"It's no excuse."

"Look, can we just do this?"

She said nothing. He stepped into her bathroom and ran the faucet until the water was warm, then filled a mixing bowl halfway full. He pumped a few dollops of soap into it, and dropped a washcloth in. Returning to his mother, he knelt before her and pulled the blanket from her legs. She wore old cotton underwear and nothing else, permitting easy access to her thin, bleached legs, which ended in rough stumps just above her ankles. The calf muscles of her left leg were shaved nearly to the bone; her leg was wrapped in bandages, stained a deep rusty brown.

She touched her fingers to his back, making him jump. "You look just like your father," she said. "So handsome."

"Come on, Mom."

"No wonder this girl likes you so much."

"You don't even know that."

"No, I do. You're too much like your dad. You even sound like him."

Nick elected not to respond. He hadn't seen his father since he was a little boy, and the notion that he was growing into him, like a disease with a single prognosis, was hardly encouraging.

"Why didn't you tell me you were bringing a girl over?"

He sat there in front of her, looking at her mauled appendages.

"I think it's wonderful," she said. She pushed her right leg toward him, the nub hovering just over his right knee. Nick tried to remain stoic as he unwrapped her bandages, the gauze tugging at the scabby undergrowth. A ripe odor wafted from the wound; he closed his eyes and steadied himself against it. Blood still seeped from the place she had shaved more of herself off. He squeezed soapy water from the washcloth and applied it gently to her leg, dabbing the raw areas, wiping down in smooth, clean strokes in the places where the wounds had closed. Nick didn't cry, but that was no kind of victory; tears would be better than this numb separation.

His mother watched him while he performed these ministrations, her face graced by something like a smile.

When he was done cleaning her wounds, he applied some alcohol to her leg. Then took the bowl of bloody water back to the bathroom, where he poured it into the sink. He returned with fresh bandages, which he wrapped around the leg. His mother's hand slipped off the armrest and grasped at the empty air; Nick put his own hand into it, and she squeezed it tightly. "If I could change it all, I would, Nicky. I would."

He shook his head, though she wasn't even looking at him.

He climbed to his feet, tucking the blanket back over her ravaged legs. He noticed a plate on the floor by her bed, a smear of blood on its face. He stooped to retrieve it. He wondered what she would do when she ran out of leg. He wondered how long it had been since she'd eaten anything cooked.

I should feel something, he thought. Where is the part of me that feels?

From elsewhere in the house, they heard the sound of Nick's bedroom door opening.

Trixie's voice floated down the hall. "Nick?"

His mother touched his hand as he moved to walk by. The light from the candle she carried made of her face a study of soft golds and darkness. A Madonna in Hell's ink. "I want to meet her."

He built a smile. "We'll see, Mom."

He pushed Trixie back into his room. "What the fuck were you doing!"

"What? I was looking for you. Get your hands off me!" She slapped his arm away. "What the fuck!"

He closed the door and sat on his bed. "I'm sorry. I'm sorry."

His room was lit by the crossbeams of six or seven flashlights placed at various opposing points; the net effect was, if not complete illumination, then at least a kind of flat radiance. Though not as distressingly fetid as the rest of the house, his room was still the refuge of a fifteen-year-old boy, and cluttered even at its best. His bed was unmade; a leaning stack of CDs tottered on the edge of his bureau, comprised of bands like Hatecrime and RaHoWa and Midtown Boot Boys; posters of seventies slasher flicks and zombie epics covered the walls. He suddenly noticed that his small collection of pornographic movies, which he had neglected to hide, had been aligned in a neat row behind him across the mattress. He opened his mouth to offer an explanation that would preserve his dignity, but of course there was none. He considered braining himself into oblivion with one of the flashlights.

She leaned against the desk and looked him over. "How often do you do it?"

"What?"

"You jerk off, right? That's what these movies are for."

"Um, I don't . . . ."

"Are you embarrassed?"

He laughed too loudly. "Yeah, I guess, kinda."

"How do you like to do it? Do you use a lubricant? Spit on your hand or something?"

"Um, no." His body temperature was escalating to dangerous levels. She looked at his crotch, put her hands on her hips, and cocked her head at an angle.

"Show me."

"Come on, Trix."

"Why do you think I came here tonight? Show me."

He gave up trying to subdue his fluttering heart, hoped she wouldn't see his hands shake, wondered if she knew that he had never been with a woman before, wondered if that fact blasted from him like bright radiation. He undid his jeans and took his penis out, and began to do as she wished.

"Do it slow," she said, stepping closer. She watched for a moment, then started to unbutton her shirt. She wore nothing underneath, and she moved her shoulders so that her blouse slid behind her to the floor; she stepped out of her jeans like a woman stepping out of water. Tattoos were inscribed all over her thin flesh; their bright colors made them luminescent in the harsh glow of the flashlights: a snake coiling over her upper right arm and looped halfway down to her elbow; a naked pixie with a devil's face under her collarbone; a series of words—poems or mysterious lists—beginning at her pelvis and wrapping around her thighs; the crossed hammers over a Confederate flag on the slope of one breast; a black swastika, like a clumsy snare of stitches, on the other. They glowed on her naked body like an incandescent language. He had once heard the phrase "illuminated manuscript," and although he did not know what such a thing was, he thought that it must be something like Trixie's body, which was covered with the letters of a holy alphabet, and which was itself a supple word, or a series of words, a phrase which she whispered to him now as she moved his hand aside and replaced it with her own. She moved them toward his bed, and he abdicated himself to the study of her.


"I have fat thighs," she said. They lay atop his sheets, still naked. The event had lasted only a few awful minutes; he'd spent himself almost immediately, after which she had rolled abruptly off of him and stared at the ceiling. He wanted to get up and clean himself off, but he didn't know what the protocol was. He felt scooped out, doomed, as though he had seen an emptiness behind the face of things. So he followed her direction and just lay there silently, until this revelation.

He craned his neck and looked down at her thighs. But his attention, despite his honest effort, was drawn powerfully away from them. "They look all right," he said.

"I got 'em from my mom. There's nothing I can do about it." She popped her hands against them, making them shake. "Fuck," she said.

"Hey, stop. You're beautiful."

"Yeah, whatever. Derrick says they're good for the movement, though."

"He said what?"

"Big thighs. You know. Child-bearing hips. It's our duty to produce pure white babies."

"Oh." He imagined Derrick examining her hips, running his hands over them. He was pretty sure Derrick lasted a lot longer than two or three minutes.

"It's funny when you think about it," Trixie said. "The things we pass on to our kids. I got my mother's elephant thighs, which sucks, but I also got my pure blood. Which is, you know, really fucking important. And which I gotta pass on, too. So I guess you can't complain too much."

Nick watched the ceiling. They had turned off all but one of the flashlights, which burned like a star in the far corner. Everything in the room threw an exaggerated shadow. "How many kids do you want to have?"

"Five or six, I guess. We got to. White people are the minority now. We're losing our country. It's my duty to have lots a kids."

Nick tried to imagine being a father. He didn't know what fathers acted like, what they looked like or how they spoke. "I don't know if I could do it," he said.

"You'd make a good dad. You're sweet."

It was not the word he was hoping to hear moments after losing his virginity.

"What did you get from your parents?" Trixie said.

"I don't think anything," he responded after a moment's consideration.

"You had to get something. Your looks, the way you act. It's kinda weird, the only way you might get to know something about your dad is through the kind of man you grow into. It's like a special hidden message he left you, or something."

Nick decided fuck the protocol, he was getting up. "I gotta get out of here," he said, jumping out of bed and fishing for his clothes.

"I'm getting at something though, Nickie."

He stopped. "What."

"Responsibility. Heritage. You can't just be selfish anymore. You got to decide who you are, and what you owe your family."

"What family."

"The one you already have, and more importantly the one you're going to have."

"You want me to prove something to the Hammers."

"Why don't you start by proving something to me? I need you to be more than just a sweet boy, Nickie. There has to be more than that."

Nick didn't look at her as he dressed. "Do you have a gun?" he asked.

She clearly hadn't been expecting that. She stared at him for a moment. "I can get one," she said.


Tyrone still lived with his mother. Nick had overheard him talking about it to Big Jake one day, how she worked second shift out at a hotel by the university on Elysian Fields, and he had to pick her up every night at ten and drive her back home. It was still not quite nine; it would be a simple thing to stake the place out and follow them home. In fact, all of it would be simple. He'd shot a rat once, when he was a kid stalking the neighborhood with a BB gun. He didn't think this could be much different.

Trixie was the only one who summoned any feeling from him anymore. He would do anything it took. If it took something grandly catastrophic, all the better. Maybe he would feel that, too.

While they had been inside, the sky had really opened up. By the time Trixie drove them through the torrential rain to Matt's house in Midcity, it was well past nine o'clock.

"We need a gun," she said to Matt after he ushered them inside. Matt was dressed in boxer shorts and nothing else. He sat on the edge of the couch and stared at the TV, which was showing some war movie.

"You wanna beer?" he asked Trixie. He had not looked at Nick even once.

"No thanks."

"What you need a gun for?"

Nick waited for Trixie to explain it to him, but when she remained silent, he knew the question was meant for him.

"I need to shoot somebody," he said.

"No shit." He kept watching the TV.

"I'm ready to do my duty."

That seemed to get through, but not in the way he wanted. Matt looked up at him with naked contempt. "By shootin some nigger? All that's gonna do is get you thrown in jail. Next thing my ass is right there with you. Get the fuck out of here, dude."

"I won't get caught."

"Not with my gun you won't."

Trixie spoke up. "I know you got some disposables here," she said.

"Why don't you shut the fuck up, Trix?"

"This is what Derrick wants, Matt. Come on."

Nick stared at her, suddenly off-kilter. When had Derrick become a factor in this?

"Well, he didn't mention it to me," Matt said, looking back at the TV. He seemed unaccountably engrossed in a commercial for an electric razor.

"There's a lot he don't mention to you," Trixie said coolly. "Not to any of you. Not unless you been climbin in bed with him . . . but I don't remember seein you there."

Something in Nick's chest dropped; he felt suddenly heavy, and wondered if he would be able to move if he had to. Matt stewed silently for a few minutes, then cursed under his breath and went into the bedroom. He came back a few moments later with a small black piece of metal wrapped in a washcloth. He handed it directly to Trixie, and said, "This is on you. If things get fucked up, it's on you."

She took the gun from him. "You act like I don't know what I'm doing." She turned for the door. Nick turned to follow, but Matt said, "Hey." When Nick looked at him, he smiled. "So, how does Derrick's dick taste?"

Matt was still laughing when Nick shut the door.

Streams of water flowed along the passenger window as the car sped down a raised stretch of I-10, and behind the water the city flowed by too, bejeweled with light, like a dream of an enchanted kingdom. Nick leaned his head against the glass and tried to pretend he was somewhere else, somewhere far from this city and the people who lived in it, somewhere you didn't have to fight a war every day to justify who you were. Trixie sat beside him, steering the car through the rain, her fingers clenching the wheel like it was a lifeline.

"What about his mother?" she said, breaking his lovely illusion.

"I don't know," Nick said. "I hadn't really thought about it."

"Well, now's a good time to start."

He decided not to respond. Trixie nodded, thinking her own thoughts. The rain increased its intensity, and she clicked the windshield wipers on high. New Orleans was behind them now; Nick had to look in the side mirror to see it. The deluge slowed the traffic, making the rain seem even heavier. Headlights from cars in the opposite lane smeared across the windshield, growing and fading like pulsars.

"You knew I was with him," Trixie said.

"*Was*, I knew you *was* with him! I didn't know you came straight from his fucking house!"

"I didn't."

"Well—*whatever*, Trixie! What the fuck!"

"It's not like I'm his girlfriend or anything, okay? We just fuck sometimes. It's no big deal."

"Right, no big deal."

"Oh, fucking grow up, would you?"

A green BMW cut in front of them and Trixie stepped on the brakes. The tires locked for a moment and the car hydroplaned nearly halfway across the lane before it regained traction.

"Motherfucker!" she said, lips peeling back from her teeth.

"You want me to drive?"

"No, I don't want you to drive."

"You sure?"

"Nick! I can drive the goddamned car!"

The BMW in front of them veered to the right and accelerated down the highway. Someone leaned on a horn. A pick-up truck eased into the vacant spot, pulling a horse trailer. Nick could see the animal's vague white shape inside, and he wondered where it needed to go in all this rain, what urgency compelled it.

After a few moments, he said, "Did you even want to sleep with me? Or were you just following orders?"

"Nick . . ."

Tires squealed on the pavement somewhere ahead of them, followed by the dull, muted thud of crumpling metal. Red brake lights splashed over the beaded water on the windshield. The pick-up swerved to the right, but it moved too quickly and the horse trailer yawed over on its left wheels and for one moment it seemed to freeze there, as though weighing consequences, and beyond it Nick saw the green BMW on its roof, its wheels sending gleaming arcs of water into the sky as they spun, and another car further ahead with its front end crushed against the concrete divider in the middle of the highway. Then the horse trailer fell, sending a rooster-tail of sparks into the air; the walls came loose, and the horse careened along the pavement in a grotesque tumble of limbs and flying hair, until it collided with the BMW and stopped.

Trixie hit the brakes and the car spun in a half circle, sliding across the lanes until the rear bumper hit the divider with the sound of breaking glass and folding metal, and they stopped. The car faced backwards; they watched approaching regiments of headlights ease to a slow crawl.

They breathed heavily for a few moments, hearing nothing but the drumming rain. A burnt, metallic odor filled the car. Someone outside started to scream.

Nick grabbed Trixie and turned her face towards him. "Trix? Are you okay?" She nodded, dazed. He felt blood on his own face, and reached up to feel a small split between his eyes; apparently he'd hit the dashboard. He looked out the back window at the accident's aftermath and said, "Stay here."

He opened the passenger door and climbed out into a cold brace of air. The rain was a frozen weight, soaking his clothes instantly. A confused array of lights speared through the rain, giving the scene a freakish radiance. He noticed that he was casting several shadows.

The horse's big body jerked as it tried to right itself, and Nick heard bones crack somewhere inside it. The horse screamed. It lay next to the overturned car, amidst a glittering galaxy of broken glass, its legs crooked and snapped, its blood spilling onto the asphalt and trailing away in diluted rivers. It was beautiful, even in these awful circumstances; its body seemed phosphorescent in the rain.

Nick knelt beside it and brushed his fingers against its skin. The flesh jumped, and he was overwhelmed by a powerful scent of urine and musk. Its eye rolled to look at him. Nick stared back, paralyzed. The horse's blood pooled around his shoe. It seemed an astonishing end for this animal, that it should come to die on some hard ground its ancestors never knew, surrounded by machines they never dreamed. Its absurdity offended him.

Someone splashed by him and dropped to his knees, peering into the overturned BMW; he shouted *Oh my God, oh my God,* and tugged frantically, futilely, at its door. Nick sensed a larger movement around him as people left their cars and began shouting, milling around the scene in a vortex of chaos and adrenaline.

"Nick!"

Trixie materialized behind him and pulled at his shoulders.

"Come on, we have to get out of here!"

He came to his feet.

"Nick, let's go. The police are coming. We can't get caught with that gun."

The gun. Nick brushed roughly past her, nearly knocking her to her knees. He retrieved the gun from her glove compartment and headed back to the horse. Trixie intercepted him, tried to push him back. "No, no, are you fucking crazy? It's gonna die anyway!"

He wrenched her aside, and this time she did fall. He walked over to the horse and the gun cracked twice, two bright flashes in the rain, and the horse was dead. A kind of peace settled over him then, a floating calm, and he stuffed the gun into his trousers, ignoring the heat of the barrel pressing into his flesh. Trixie had not bothered to get up from the pavement. She sat there, watching him, the rain sluicing over her head and down her body. Her face was inscrutable behind the curtain of rain, as was everything else about her. He left her there.

Behind her, the car was hopelessly ensnared in the traffic jam. He would have to walk home, to his mother, broken and beautiful, crashed in her own foreign landscape. Bewildered and terrified. Burning love

like a gasoline. He started down the highway, walking along the edge
of stopped traffic. He felt the weightlessness of mercy. He was a
striding christ. Sounds filtered through to him: people yelling and
pleading; footsteps splashing through the rain; a distant, stranded
siren. From somewhere behind him a man's sob, weird and ululating,
rose above the wreckage and disappeared into the sky, a flaming rag.

# The Crevasse

(with Dale Bailey)

*What he loved was the silence, the pristine* clarity of the ice shelf: the purposeful breathing of the dogs straining against their traces, the hiss of the runners, the opalescent arc of the sky. Garner peered through shifting veils of snow at the endless sweep of glacial terrain before him, the wind gnawing at him, forcing him to reach up periodically and scrape at the thin crust of ice that clung to the edges of his facemask, the dry rasp of the fabric against his face reminding him that he was alive.

There were fourteen of them. Four men, one of them, Faber, strapped to the back of Garner's sledge, mostly unconscious, but occasionally surfacing out of the morphine depths to moan. Ten dogs, big Greenland huskies, gray and white. Two sledges. And the silence, scouring him of memory and desire, hollowing him out inside. It was what he'd come to Antarctica for.

And then, abruptly, the silence split open like a wound:

A thunderous crack, loud as lightning cleaving stone, shivered the ice, and the dogs of the lead sledge, maybe twenty-five yards ahead of Garner, erupted into panicky cries. Garner saw it happen: the lead sledge sloughed over—hurling Connelly into the snow—and plunged nose first through the ice, as though an enormous hand had reached up through the earth to snatch it under. Startled, he watched an instant longer. The wrecked sledge, jutting out of the earth like a broken stone, hurtled at him, closer, closer. Then time stuttered, leaping forward. Garner flung one of the brakes out behind him. The hook skittered over the ice. Garner felt the jolt in his spine when it caught. Rope sang out behind him, arresting his momentum. But it wouldn't be enough.

Garner flung out a second brake, then another. The hooks snagged, jerking the sledge around and up on a single runner. For a moment Garner thought that it was going to roll, dragging the dogs along behind it. Then the airborne runner slammed back to earth and the sledge skidded to a stop in a glittering spray of ice.

Dogs boiled back into its shadow, howling and snapping. Ignoring them, Garner clambered free. He glanced back at Faber, still miraculously strapped to the travois, his face ashen, and then he pelted toward the wrecked sledge, dodging a minefield of spilled cargo: food and tents, cooking gear, his medical bag, disgorging a bright freight of tools and the few precious ampules of morphine McReady had been willing to spare, like a fan of scattered diamonds.

The wrecked sledge hung precariously, canted on a lip of ice above a black crevasse. As Garner stood there, it slipped an inch, and then another, dragged down by the weight of the dogs. He could hear them whining, claws scrabbling as they strained against harnesses drawn taut by the weight of Atka, the lead dog, dangling out of sight beyond the edge of the abyss.

Garner visualized him—thrashing against his tack in a black well as the jagged circle of grayish light above shrank away, inch by lurching inch—and he felt the pull of night inside himself, the age-old gravity of the dark. Then a hand closed around his ankle.

Bishop, clinging to the ice, a hand-slip away from tumbling into the crevasse himself: face blanched, eyes red rimmed inside his goggles.

"Shit," Garner said. "Here—"

He reached down, locked his hand around Bishop's wrist, and hauled him up, boots slipping. Momentum carried him over backwards, floundering in the snow as Bishop curled fetal beside him.

"You okay?"

"My ankle," he said through gritted teeth.

"Here, let me see."

"Not now. Connelly. What happened to Connelly?"

"He fell off—"

With a metallic screech, the sledge broke loose. It slid a foot, a foot and a half, and then it hung up. The dogs screamed. Garner had never heard a dog make a noise like that—he didn't know dogs *could* make a noise like that—and for a moment their blind, inarticulate terror swam through him. He thought again of Atka, dangling there, turning, feet clawing at the darkness, and he felt something stir inside him once again—

"Steady, man," Bishop said.

Garner drew in a long breath, icy air lacerating his lungs.

"You gotta be steady now, Doc," Bishop said. "You gotta go cut him loose."

"No—"

"We're gonna lose the sledge. And the rest of the team. That happens, we're all gonna die out here, okay? I'm busted up right now, I need you to do this thing—"

"What about Connell—"

"Not now, Doc. Listen to me. We don't have time. Okay?"

Bishop held his gaze. Garner tried to look away, could not. The other man's eyes fixed him.

"Okay," he said.

Garner stood and stumbled away. Went to his knees to dig through the wreckage. Flung aside a sack of rice, frozen in clumps, wrenched open a crate of flares—useless—shoved it aside, and dragged another one toward him. This time he was lucky: he dug out a coil of rope, a hammer, a handful of pitons. The sledge lurched on its lip of ice, the rear end swinging, setting off another round of whimpering.

"Hurry," Bishop said.

Garner drove the pitons deep into the permafrost and threaded the rope through their eyes, his hands stiff inside his gloves. Lashing the other end around his waist, he edged back onto the broken ice shelf. It shifted underneath him, creaking. The sledge shuddered, but held. Below him, beyond the moiling clump of dogs, he could see the leather trace leads, stretched taut across the jagged rim of the abyss.

He dropped back, letting rope out as he descended. The world fell away above him. Down and down, and then he was on his knees at the very edge of the shelf, the hot, rank stink of the dogs enveloping him. He used his teeth to loosen one glove. Working quickly against the icy assault of the elements, he fumbled his knife out of its sheath and pressed the blade to the first of the traces. He sawed at it until the leather separated with a snap.

Atka's weight shifted in the darkness below him, and the dog howled mournfully. Garner set to work on the second trace, felt it let go, everything—the sledge, the terrified dogs—slipping toward darkness. For a moment he thought the whole thing would go. But it held. He went to work on the third trace, gone loose now by some trick of tension. It too separated beneath his blade, and he once again felt Atka's weight shift in the well of darkness beneath him.

Garner peered into the blackness. He could see the dim blur of the dog, could feel its dumb terror welling up around him, and as he brought the blade to the final trace, a painstakingly erected dike gave way in his mind. Memory flooded through him: the feel of mangled flesh beneath his fingers, the distant whump of artillery, Elizabeth's drawn and somber face.

His fingers faltered. Tears blinded him. The sledge shifted above him as Atka thrashed in his harness. Still he hesitated.

The rope creaked under the strain of additional weight. Ice rained down around him. Garner looked up to see Connelly working his way hand over hand down the rope.

"Do it," Connelly grunted, his eyes like chips of flint. "Cut him loose."

Garner's fingers loosened around the hilt of the blade. He felt the tug of the dark at his feet, Atka whining.

"Give me the goddamn knife," Connelly said, wrenching it away, and together they clung there on the single narrow thread of gray rope, two men and one knife and the enormous gulf of the sky overhead as Connelly sawed savagely at the last of the traces. It held for a moment, and then, abruptly, it gave, loose ends curling back and away from the blade.

Atka fell howling into darkness.


They made camp.

The traces of the lead sledge had to be untangled and repaired, the dogs tended to, the weight redistributed to account for Atka's loss. While Connelly busied himself with these chores, Garner stabilized Faber—the blood had frozen to a black crust inside the makeshift splint Garner had applied yesterday, after the accident—and wrapped Bishop's ankle. These were automatic actions. Serving in France he'd learned the trick of letting his body work while his mind traveled to other places; it had been crucial to keeping his sanity during the war, when the people brought to him for treatment had been butchered by German submachine guns or burned and blistered by mustard gas. He worked to save those men, though it was hopeless work. Mankind had acquired an appetite for dying; doctors were merely shepherds to the process. Surrounded by screams and spilled blood, he'd anchored himself to memories of his wife, Elizabeth: the warmth of her kitchen back home in Boston, and the warmth of her body, too.

But all that was gone.

Now, when he let his mind wander, it went to dark places, and he found himself concentrating instead on the minutiae of these rote tasks like a first-year medical student. He cut a length of bandage and applied a compression wrap to Bishop's exposed ankle, covering both ankle and foot in careful figure-eights. He kept his mind in the moment, listening to the harsh labor of their lungs in the frigid air, to Connelly's chained fury as he worked at the traces, and to the muffled sounds of the dogs as they burrowed into the snow to rest.

And he listened, too, to Atka's distant cries, leaking from the crevasse like blood.

"Can't believe that dog's still alive," Bishop said, testing his ankle against his weight. He grimaced and sat down on a crate. "He's a tough old bastard."

Garner imagined Elizabeth's face, drawn tight with pain and determination, while he fought a war on the far side of the ocean. Was she afraid too, suspended over her own dark hollow? Did she cry out for him?

"Help me with this tent," Garner said.

They'd broken off from the main body of the expedition to bring Faber back to one of the supply depots on the Ross Ice Shelf, where Garner could care for him. They would wait there for the remainder of the expedition, which suited Garner just fine, but troubled both Bishop and Connelly, who had higher aspirations for their time here.

Nightfall was still a month away, but if they were going to camp here while they made repairs, they would need the tents to harvest warmth. Connelly approached as they drove pegs into the permafrost, his eyes impassive as they swept over Faber, still tied down to the travois, locked inside a morphine dream. He regarded Bishop's ankle and asked him how it was.

"It'll do," Bishop said. "It'll have to. How are the dogs?"

"We need to start figuring what we can do without," Connelly said. "We're gonna have to leave some stuff behind."

"We're only down one dog," Bishop said. "It shouldn't be too hard to compensate."

"We're down two. One of the swing dogs snapped her foreleg." He opened one of the bags lashed to the rear sledge, removing an Army-issue revolver. "So go ahead and figure what we don't need.

I gotta tend to her." He tossed a contemptuous glance at Garner. "Don't worry, I won't ask you to do it."

Garner watched as Connelly approached the injured dog, lying away from the others in the snow. She licked obsessively at her broken leg. As Connelly approached she looked up at him, and her tail wagged weakly. Connelly aimed the pistol and fired a bullet through her head. The shot made a flat, inconsequential sound, swallowed up by the vastness of the open plain.

Garner turned away, emotion surging through him with a surprising, disorienting energy. Bishop met his gaze and offered a rueful smile.

"Bad day," he said.


Still, Atka whimpered.

Garner lay wakeful, staring at the canvas, taut and smooth as the interior of an egg above him. Faber moaned, calling out after some fever phantom. Garner almost envied the man. Not the injury—a nasty compound fracture of the femur, the product of a bad step on the ice when he'd stepped outside the circle of tents to piss—but the sweet oblivion of the morphine doze.

In France, in the war, he'd known plenty of doctors who'd used the stuff to chase away the night haunts. He'd also seen the fevered agony of withdrawal. He had no wish to experience that, but he felt the opiate lure all the same. He'd felt it then, when he'd had thoughts of Elizabeth to sustain him. And he felt it now—stronger still— when he didn't.

Elizabeth had fallen victim to the greatest cosmic prank of all time, the flu that had swept across the world in the spring and summer of 1918, as if the bloody abattoir in the trenches hadn't been evidence enough of humanity's divine disfavor. That's what Elizabeth had called it in the last letter he'd ever had from her: God's judgment on a world gone mad. Garner had given up on God by then: he'd packed away the Bible Elizabeth had pressed upon him after a week in the field hospital, knowing that its paltry lies could bring him no comfort in the face of such horror, and it hadn't. Not then, and not later, when he'd come home to face Elizabeth's mute and barren grave. Garner had taken McReady's offer to accompany the expedition soon after, and though he'd stowed the Bible in his gear before he left, he hadn't opened it since and he wouldn't open it here, either, lying sleepless beside a man who might yet die because he'd had to take a piss—yet another grand cosmic joke—in a place so hellish and forsaken that even Elizabeth's God could find no purchase here.

There could be no God in such a place.

Just the relentless shriek of the wind tearing at the flimsy canvas, and the death-howl agony of the dog. Just emptiness, and the unyielding porcelain dome of the polar sky.

Garner sat up, breathing heavily.

Faber muttered under his breath. Garner leaned over the injured man, the stench of fever hot in his nostrils. He smoothed Faber's hair back from his forehead and studied the leg, swollen tight as a sausage inside the sealskin legging. Garner didn't like to think what he might see if he slit open that sausage to reveal the leg underneath: the viscous pit of the wound itself, crimson lines of sepsis twining around Faber's thigh like a malevolent vine as they climbed inexorably toward his heart.

Atka howled, a long rising cry that broke into pitiful yelps, died away, and renewed itself, like the shriek of sirens on the French front.

"Jesus," Garner whispered.

He fished a flask out of his pack and allowed himself a single swallow of whiskey. Then he sat in the dark, listening to the mournful lament of the dog, his mind filling with hospital images: the red splash of tissue in a steel tray, the enflamed wound of an amputation, the hand folding itself into an outraged fist as the arm fell away. He thought of Elizabeth, too, Elizabeth most of all, buried months before Garner had gotten back from Europe. And he thought of Connelly, that aggrieved look as he turned away to deal with the injured swing dog.

*Don't worry, I won't ask you to do it.*

Crouching in the low tent, Garner dressed. He shoved a flashlight into his jacket, shouldered aside the tent flap, and leaned into the wind tearing across the waste. The crevasse lay before him, rope still trailing through the pitons to dangle into the pit below.

Garner felt the pull of darkness. And Atka, screaming.

"Okay," he muttered. "All right, I'm coming."

Once again he lashed the rope around his waist. This time he didn't hesitate as he backed out onto the ledge of creaking ice. Hand over hand he went, backward and down, boots scuffing until he stepped into space and hung suspended in a well of shadow.

Panic seized him, the black certainty that nothing lay beneath him. The crevasse yawned under his feet, like a wedge of vacuum driven into the heart of the planet. Then, below him—ten feet? twenty?— Atka mewled, piteous as a freshly whelped pup, eyes squeezed shut against the light. Garner thought of the dog, curled in agony upon some shelf of subterranean ice, and began to lower himself into the pit, darkness rising to envelop him.

One heartbeat, then another and another and another, his breath diaphanous in the gloom, his boots scrabbling for solid ground. Scrabbling and finding it. Garner clung to the rope, testing the surface with his weight.

It held.

Garner took the flashlight from his jacket, and switched it on. Atka peered up at him, brown eyes iridescent with pain. The dog's legs twisted underneath it, and its tail wagged feebly. Blood glistened at its muzzle. As he moved closer, Garner saw that a dagger of bone had pierced its torso, unveiling the slick yellow gleam of subcutaneous fat and deeper still, half visible through tufts of coarse fur, the bloody pulse of viscera. And it had shat itself—Garner could smell it—a thin gruel congealing on the dank stone.

"Okay," he said. "Okay, Atka."

Kneeling, Garner caressed the dog. It growled and subsided, surrendering to his ministrations.

"Good boy, Atka," he whispered. "Settle down, boy."

Garner slid his knife free of its sheath, bent forward, and brought the blade to the dog's throat. Atka whimpered—"Shhh," Garner whispered—as he bore down with the edge, steeling himself against the thing he was about to do—

Something moved in the darkness beneath him: a leathery rasp, the echoing clatter of stone on stone, of loose pebbles tumbling into darkness. Atka whimpered again, legs twitching as he tried to shove himself back against the wall. Garner, startled, shoved the blade forward. Atka's neck unseamed itself in a welter of black arterial blood. The dog stiffened, shuddered once, and died—Garner watched its eyes dim in the space of a single heartbeat—and once again something shifted in the darkness at Garner's back. Garner scuttled backward, slamming his shoulders into the wall by Atka's corpse. He froze there, probing the darkness.

Then, when nothing came—had he imagined it? He must have imagined it—Garner aimed the flashlight light into the gloom. His breath caught in his throat. He shoved himself erect in amazement, the rope pooling at his feet.

Vast.

The place was vast: walls of naked stone climbing in cathedral arcs to the undersurface of the polar plain and a floor worn smooth as glass over long ages, stretching out before him until it dropped away into an abyss of darkness. Struck dumb with terror—or was it wonder?—Garner stumbled forward, the rope unspooling behind him until he drew up at the precipice, pointed the light into the shadows before him, and saw what it was that he had discovered.

A stairwell, cut seamlessly into the stone itself, and no human stairwell either: each riser fell away three feet or more, the stair itself winding endlessly into fathomless depths of earth, down and down and down until it curved away beyond the reach of his frail human light, and further still toward some awful destination he scarcely dared imagine. Garner felt the lure and hunger of the place singing in his bones. Something deep inside him, some mute inarticulate longing, cried out in response, and before he knew it he found himself scrambling down the first riser and then another, the flashlight carving slices out of the darkness to reveal a bas-relief of inhuman creatures lunging at him in glimpses: taloned feet and clawed hands and sinuous Medusa coils that seemed to writhe about one another in the fitful and imperfect glare. And through it all the terrible summons of the place, drawing him down into the dark.

"Elizabeth—" he gasped, stumbling down another riser and another, until the rope, forgotten, jerked taut about his waist. He looked up at the pale circle of Connelly's face far above him.

"What the hell are you doing down there, Doc?" Connelly shouted, his voice thick with rage, and then, almost against his will, Garner found himself ascending once again into the light.

No sooner had he gained his footing than Connelly grabbed him by the collar and swung him to the ground. Garner scrabbled for purchase in the snow but Connelly kicked him back down again, his blond, bearded face contorted in rage.

"You stupid son of a bitch! Do you care if we all die out here?"

"Get off me!"

"For a dog? For a goddamned *dog?*" Connelly tried to kick him again, but Garner grabbed his foot and rolled, bringing the other man down on top of him. The two of them grappled in the snow, their heavy coats and gloves making any real damage impossible.

The flaps to one of the tents opened and Bishop limped out, his face a caricature of alarm. He was buttoning his coat even as he approached. "Stop! *Stop it right now!*"

Garner clambered to his feet, staggering backward a few steps. Connelly rose to one knee, leaning over and panting. He pointed at Garner. "I found him in the crevasse! He went down alone!"

Garner leaned against one of the packed sledges. He could feel Bishop watching him as tugged free a glove to poke at a tender spot on his face, but he didn't look up.

"Is this true?"

"Of course it's true!" Connelly said, but Bishop waved him into silence.

Garner looked up at him, breath heaving in his lungs. "You've got to see it," he said. "My God, Bishop."

Bishop turned his gaze to the crevasse, where he saw the pitons and the rope spilling into the darkness. "Oh, Doc," he said quietly.

"It's not a crevasse, Bishop. It's a stairwell."

Connelly strode toward Garner, jabbing his finger at him. "What? You lost your goddamned mind."

"Look for yourself!"

Bishop interposed himself between the two men. "Enough!" He turned to face Connelly. "Back off."

"But—"

"I said back off!" Connelly peeled his lips back, then turned and stalked back toward the crevasse. He knelt by its edge and started hauling up the rope.

Bishop turned to Garner. "Explain yourself."

All at once, Garner's passion drained from him. He felt a wash of exhaustion. His muscles ached. How could he explain this to him? How could he explain this so that they'd understand? "Atka," he said simply, imploringly. "I could hear him."

A look of deep regret fell over Bishop's face. "Doc . . . Atka was a just a dog. We have to get Faber to the depot."

"I could still hear him."

"You have to pull yourself together. There are real lives at stake here, do you get that? Me and Connelly, we aren't doctors. Faber needs *you*."

"But—"

"Do you get that?"

"I . . . yeah. Yeah, I know."

"When you go down into places like that, especially by yourself, you're putting us all at risk. What are we gonna do without Doc, huh?"

This was not an argument Garner would win. Not this way. So he grabbed Bishop by the arm and led him toward the crevasse. "Look," he said.

Bishop wrenched his arm free, his face darkening. Connelly straightened, watching this exchange. "Don't put your hands on me, Doc," Bishop said.

"Bishop," Garner said. "Please."

Bishop paused a moment, then walked toward the opening. "All right."

Connelly exploded. "Oh for Christ's sake!"

"We're not going inside it," Bishop said, looking at them both. "I'm going to look, okay, Doc? That's all you get."

Garner nodded. "Okay," he said. "Okay."

The two of them approached the edge of the crevasse. Closer, Garner felt it like a hook in his liver, tugging him down. It took an act of will to stop at the edge, to remain still and unshaken and look at these other two men as if his whole life did not hinge upon this moment.

"It's a stairwell," he said. His voice did not shake. His body did not move. "It's carved into the rock. It's got . . . designs of some kind." Bishop peered down into the darkness for a long moment. "I don't see anything," he said at last.

"I'm telling you, it's *there!*" Garner stopped and gathered himself. He tried another tack. "This, this could be the scientific discovery of the century. You want to stick it to McReady? Let him plant his little flag. This is evidence of, of . . ." He trailed off. He didn't know what it was evidence of.

"We'll mark the location," Bishop said. "We'll come back. If what you say is true, it's not going anywhere."

Garner switched on his flashlight. "Look," he said, and he threw it down.

The flashlight arced end over end, its white beam slicing through the darkness with a scalpel's clean efficiency, illuminating flashes of hewn rock and what might have been carvings or just natural irregularities. It clattered to a landing beside the corpse of the dog, casting in bright relief its open jaw and lolling tongue, and the black pool of blood beneath it.

Bishop looked for a moment, and shook his head. "God damn it, Doc," he said. "You're really straining my patience. Come on."

Bishop was about to turn away when Atka's body jerked once—Garner saw it—and then again, almost imperceptibly. Reaching out, Garner seized Bishop's sleeve. "What now, for Christ's—" the other man started to say, his voice harsh with annoyance. Then the body was yanked into the surrounding darkness so quickly it seemed as though it had vanished into thin air. Only its blood, a smeared trail into shadow, testified to its ever having been there at all. That, and the jostled flashlight, which rolled in a lazy half circle, its unobstructed light spearing first into empty darkness and then into smooth cold stone before settling at last on what might have been a carven, clawed foot. The beam flickered and went out.

"What the fuck . . . ," Bishop said. A scream erupted from the tent behind them. Faber.

Garner broke into a clumsy run, high-stepping through the piled snow. The other men shouted behind him, but their words were lost in the wind and in his own hard breathing. His body was moving according to its training but his mind was pinned like a writhing insect in the hole behind him, in the stark, burning image of what he had just seen. He was transported by fear and adrenaline and by something else, by some other emotion he had not felt in many years or perhaps ever in his life, some heart-filling glorious exaltation that threatened to snuff him out like a dying cinder.

Faber was sitting upright in the tent—it stank of sweat and urine and kerosene, eye-watering and sharp—his thick hair a dark corona around his head, his skin as pale as a cavefish. He was still trying to scream, but his voice had broken, and his utmost effort could now produce only a long, cracked wheeze, which seemed forced through his throat like steel wool. His leg stuck out of the blanket, still grossly swollen.

The warmth from the Nansen cooker was almost oppressive.

Garner dropped to his knees beside him and tried to ease him back down into his sleeping bag, but Faber resisted. He fixed his eyes on Garner, his painful wheeze trailing into silence. Hooking his fingers in Garner's collar, he pulled him close, so close that Garner could smell the sour taint of his breath.

"Faber, relax, relax!"

"It—" Faber's voice locked. He swallowed and tried again. "It laid an egg in me."

Bishop and Connelly crowded through the tent flap, and Garner felt suddenly hemmed in, overwhelmed by the heat and the stink and the steam rising in wisps from their clothes as they pushed closer, staring down at Faber.

"What's going on?" Bishop asked. "Is he all right?"

Faber eyed them wildly. Ignoring them, Garner placed his hands on Faber's cheeks and turned his head toward him. "Look at me, Faber. Look at me. What do you mean?"

Faber found a way to smile. "In my dream. It put my head inside its body, and it laid an egg in me."

Connelly said, "He's delirious. See what happens when you leave him alone?"

Garner fished an ampule of morphine out of his bag. Faber saw what he was doing, and his body bucked.

"No!" he screamed, summoning his voice again. "No!" His leg thrashed out, knocking over the Nansen cooker. Cursing, Connelly dove at the overturned stove, but it was already too late. Kerosene splashed over the blankets and supplies, engulfing the tent in flames. The men moved in a sudden tangle of panic. Bishop stumbled back out of the tent, and Connelly shoved Garner aside—Garner rolled over on his back and came to rest there—as he lunged for Faber's legs, dragging him backward. Screaming, Faber clutched at the ground to resist, but Connelly was too strong. A moment later, Faber was gone, dragging a smoldering rucksack with him.

Still inside the tent, Garner lay back, watching as the fire spread hungrily along the roof, dropping tongues of flame onto the ground, onto his own body. Garner closed his eyes as the heat gathered him up like a furnace-hearted lover.

What he felt, though, was not the fire's heat, but the cool breath of underground earth, the silence of the deep tomb buried beneath the ice shelf. The stairs descended before him, and at the bottom he heard a noise again: A woman's voice, calling for him. Wondering where he was.

Elizabeth, he called, his voice echoing off the stone. Are you there?

If only he'd gotten to see her, he thought. If only he'd gotten to bury her. To fill those beautiful eyes with dirt. To cover her in darkness.

Elizabeth, can you hear me?

Then Connelly's big arms enveloped him, and he felt the heat again, searing bands of pain around his legs and chest. It was like being wrapped in a star. "I ought to let you burn, you stupid son of a bitch," Connelly hissed, but he didn't. He lugged Garner outside— Garner opened his eyes in time to see the canvas part in front of him, like fiery curtains—and dumped him in the snow instead. The pain went away, briefly, and Garner mourned its passing. He rolled over and lifted his head. Connelly stood over him, his face twisted in disgust. Behind him the tent flickered and burned like a dropped torch.

Faber's quavering voice hung over it all, rising and falling like the wind.

Connelly tossed an ampule and a syringe onto the ground by Garner. "Faber's leg's opened up again," he said. "Go and do your job."

Garner climbed slowly to his feet, feeling the skin on his chest and legs tighten. He'd been burned; he'd have to wait until he'd tended to Faber to find out how badly.

"And then help us pack up," Bishop called as he led the dogs to their harnesses, his voice harsh and strained. "We're getting the hell out of here."

By the time they reached the depot, Faber was dead. Connelly spat into the snow and turned away to unhitch the dogs, while Garner and Bishop went inside and started a fire. Bishop started water boiling for coffee. Garner unpacked their bedclothes and dressed the cots, moving gingerly. Once the place was warm enough he undressed and surveyed the burn damage. It would leave scars.

The next morning they wrapped Faber's body and packed it in an ice locker.

After that they settled in to wait.

The ship would not return for a month yet, and though McReady's expedition was due back before then, the vagaries of Antarctic experience made that a tenuous proposition at best. In any case, they were stuck with each other for some time yet, and not even the generous stocks of the depot—a relative wealth of food and medical supplies, playing cards and books—could fully distract them from their grievances.

In the days that followed, Connelly managed to bank his anger at Garner, but it would not take much to set it off again; so Garner tried to keep a low profile. As with the trenches in France, corpses were easy to explain in Antarctica.

A couple of weeks into that empty expanse of time, while Connelly dozed on his cot and Bishop read through an old natural history magazine, Garner decided to risk broaching the subject of what had happened in the crevasse.

"You saw it," he said, quietly, so as not to wake Connelly.

Bishop took a moment to acknowledge that he'd heard him. Finally he tilted the magazine away, and sighed. "Saw what?" he said.

"You know what."

Bishop shook his head. "No," he said. "I don't. I don't know what you're talking about."

"Something was there."

Bishop said nothing. He lifted the magazine again, but his eyes were still.

"Something was down there," Garner said.

"No there wasn't."

"It pulled Atka. I know you saw it."

Bishop refused to look at him. "There's nothing there," he said, after a long silence. "Nothing. This is an empty place." He blinked, and turned a page in the magazine.

Garner leaned back onto his cot, looking at the ceiling. Although the long Antarctic day had not yet finished, it was shading into dusk, the sun hovering over the horizon like a great boiling eye. It cast long shadows, and the lamp Bishop had lit to read by set them dancing. Garner watched them caper across the ceiling. Some time later, Bishop snuffed out the lamp and dragged the curtains over the windows, consigning them all to darkness. With it, Garner felt something like peace stir inside him. He let it move through him in waves, he felt it ebb and flow with each slow pulse of his heart.

A gust of wind scattered fine crystals of snow against the window, and he found himself wondering what the night would be like in this cold country. He imagined the sky dissolving to reveal the hard vault of stars, the galaxy turning above him like a cog in a vast, unknowable engine. And behind it all, the emptiness into which men cast their prayers. It occurred to him that he could leave now, walk out into the long twilight and keep going until the earth opened beneath him and he found himself descending strange stairs, while the world around him broke silently into snow, and into night.

Garner closed his eyes.

# The Monsters of Heaven

*For a long time, Brian imagined reunions with* his son. In the early days, these fantasies were defined by spectacular violence. He would find the man who stole him and open his head with a claw hammer. The more blood he spilled, the further removed he became from his own guilt. The location would often change: a roach-haunted tenement building; an abandoned warehouse along the Tchoupitoulas wharf; a pre-fab bungalow with an American flag out front and a two-door hatchback parked in the driveway.

Sometimes the man lived alone, sometimes he had his own family. On these latter occasions Brian would cast himself as a moral executioner, spraying the walls with the kidnapper's blood but sparing his wife and child—freeing them, he imagined, from his tyranny. No matter the scenario, Toby was always there, always intact; Brian would feel his face pressed into his shoulders as he carried him away, feel the heat of his tears bleed into his shirt. You're safe now, he would say. Daddy's got you. Daddy's here.

After some months passed, he deferred the heroics to the police. This marked his first concession to reality. He spent his time beached in the living room, drinking more, working less, until the owner of the auto shop told him to take time off, a lot of time off, as much as he needed. Brian barely noticed. He waited for the red and blue disco lights of a police cruiser to illuminate the darkness outside, to give some shape and measure to the night. He waited for the phone to ring with a glad summons to the station. He played out scenarios, tried on different outcomes, guessed at his own reactions. He gained weight and lost time.

Sometimes he would get out of bed in the middle of the night, careful not to wake his wife, and get into the car. He would drive at dangerous speeds through the city, staring into the empty sockets of unlighted windows. He would get out of the car and stand in front of some of these houses, looking and listening for signs. Often, the police were called. When the officers realized who he was, they were usually as courteous as they were adamant. He'd wonder if it had been the kidnapper who called the police. He would imagine returning to those houses with a gun.

This was in the early days of what became known as the Lamentation. At this stage, most people did not know anything unusual was happening. What they heard, if they heard anything, was larded with rumor and embellishment. Fogs of gossip in the barrooms and churches. This was before the bloodshed. Before their pleas to Christ clotted in their throats.

Amy never told Brian that she blamed him. She elected, rather, to avoid the topic of the actual abduction, and any question of her husband's negligence. Once the police abandoned them as suspects, the matter of their own involvement ceased to be a subject of discussion. Brian was unconsciously grateful, because it allowed him to focus instead on the maintenance of grief. Silence spread between them like a glacier. In a few months, entire days passed with nothing said between them.

It was on such a night that Amy rolled up against him and kissed the back of his neck. It froze Brian, filling him with a blast of terror and bewilderment; he felt the guilt move inside of him, huge but seemingly distant, like a whale passing beneath a boat. Her lips felt hot against his skin, sending warm waves rolling from his neck and shoulders all the way down to his legs, as though she had injected something lovely into him. She grew more ardent, nipping him with her teeth, breaking through his reservations. He turned and kissed her. He experienced a leaping arc of energy, a terrifying, violent impulse; he threw his weight onto her and crushed his mouth into hers, scraping his teeth against hers. But there immediately followed a cascade of unwelcome thought: Toby whimpering somewhere in the dark, waiting for his father to save him; Amy, dressed in her bed-clothes in the middle of the day, staring like a corpse into the sunlight coming through the windows; the playground, and the receding line of kindergarteners. When she reached under the sheets she found him limp and unready. He opened his mouth to apologize but she shoved her tongue into it, her hand working at him with a rough urgency, as though more depended on this than he knew. Later he would learn that it did. Her teeth sliced his lip and blood eeled into his mouth. She was pulling at him too hard, and it was starting to hurt. He wrenched himself away.

"Jesus," he said, wiping his lip. The blood felt like an oil slick in the back of his throat.

She turned her back to him and put her face into the pillow. For a moment he thought she was crying. But only for a moment.

"Honey," he said. "Hey." He put his fingers on her shoulder; she rolled it away from him.

"Go to sleep," she said.

He stared at the landscape of her naked back, pale in the street-light leaking through the blinds, feeling furious and ruined.

❦

The next morning, when he came into the kitchen, Amy was already up. Coffee was made, filling the room with a fine toasted smell, and she was leaning against the counter with a cup in her hand, wearing her pink terrycloth robe. Her dark hair was still wet from the shower. She smiled and said, "Good morning."

"Hey," he said, feeling for a sense of her mood.

Dodger, Toby's dog, cast him a devastated glance from his customary place beneath the kitchen table. Amy had wanted to get rid of him—she couldn't bear the sight of him anymore, she'd said—but Brian wouldn't allow it. When Toby comes back, he reasoned, he'll wonder why we did it. What awful thing guided us. So Dodger remained, and his slumping, sorrowful presence tore into them both like a hungry animal.

"Hey boy," Brian said, and rubbed his neck with his toe.

"I'm going out today," Amy said.

"Okay. Where to?"

She shrugged. "I don't know. The hardware store. Maybe a nursery. I want to find myself a project."

Brian looked at her. The sunlight made a corona around her body. This new resolve, coupled with her overture of the night before, struck him as a positive sign. "Okay," he said.

He seated himself at the table. The newspaper had been placed there for him, still bound by a rubberband. He snapped it off and unfurled the front page. Already he felt the gravitational pull of the Jack Daniels in the cabinet, but when Amy leaned over his shoulder and placed a coffee cup in front of him, he managed to resist the whiskey's call with an ease that surprised and gratified him. He ran his hand up her forearm, pushing back the soft pink sleeve, and he kissed the inside of her wrist. He felt a wild and incomprehensible hope. He breathed in the clean, scented smell of her. She stayed there for a moment, and then gently pulled away.

They remained that way in silence for some time—maybe fifteen minutes or more—until Brian found something in the paper he

wanted to share with her. Something being described as "angelic"—
"apparently not quite a human man," as the writer put it—had been
found down by the Gulf Coast, in Morgan City; it had been shedding a faint light from under two feet of water; whatever it was had
died shortly after being taken into custody, under confusing circumstances. He turned in his chair to speak, a word already gathering on
his tongue, and he caught her staring at him. She had a cadaverous,
empty look, as though she had seen the worst thing in the world and
died in the act. It occurred to him that she had been looking at him
that way for whole minutes. He turned back to the table, his insides
sliding, and stared at the suddenly indecipherable glyphs of the newspaper. After a moment he felt her hand on the back of his neck,
rubbing him gently. She left the kitchen without a word.


This is how it happened:

They were taking Dodger for a walk. Toby liked to hold the
leash—he was four years old, and gravely occupied with establishing
his independence—and more often than not Brian would sort of
half-trot behind them, one hand held partially outstretched should
Dodger suddenly decide to break into a run, dragging his boy behind
him like a string of tin cans. He probably bit off more profanities
during those walks than he ever did changing a tire. He carried, as was
their custom on Mondays, a blanket and a picnic lunch. He would
lie back in the sun while Toby and the dog played, and enjoy not
being hunched over an engine block. At some point they would have
lunch. Brian believed these afternoons of easy camaraderie would
be remembered by them both for years to come. They'd done it a
hundred times.

A hundred times.

On that day a kindergarten class arrived shortly after they did.
Toby ran up to his father and wrapped his arms around his neck,
frightened by the sudden bright surge of humanity; the kids were a

loud, brawling tumult, crashing over the swings and monkey bars in a gabbling surf. Brian pried Toby's arms free and pointed at them.

"Look, screwball, they're just kids. See? They're just like you. Go on and play. Have some fun."

Dodger galloped out to greet them and was received as a hero, with joyful cries and grasping fingers. Toby observed this gambit for his dog's affections and at last decided to intervene. He ran toward them, shouting, "That's my dog! That's my dog!" Brian watched him go, made eye contact with the teacher and nodded hello. She smiled at him—he remembered thinking she was kind of cute, wondering how old she was—and she returned her attention to her kids, gamboling like lunatics all over the park. Brian reclined on the blanket and watched the clouds skim the atmosphere, listened to the sound of children. It was a hot, windless day.

He didn't realize he had dozed until the kindergarteners had been rounded up and were halfway down the block, taking their noise with them. The silence stirred him.

He sat up abruptly and looked around. The playground was empty. "Toby? Hey, Toby?"

Dodger stood out in the middle of the road, his leash spooled at his feet. He watched Brian eagerly, offered a tentative wag.

"Where's Toby?" he asked the dog, and climbed to his feet. He felt a sudden sickening lurch in his gut. He turned in a quick circle, a half-smile on his face, utterly sure that this was an impossible situation, that children didn't disappear in broad daylight while their parents were *right fucking there*. So he was still here. Of course he was still here. Dodger trotted up to him and sat down at his feet, waiting for him to produce the boy, as though he were a hidden tennis ball.

"Toby?"

The park was empty. He jogged after the receding line of kids. "Hey. *Hey!* Is my son with you? *Where's my son?*"

*✢♥*

One morning, about a week after the experience in the kitchen, Brian was awakened by the phone. Every time this happened he felt a thrill of hope, though by now it had become muted, even dreadful in its predictability. He hauled himself up from the couch, nearly overturning a bottle of Jack Daniels stationed on the floor. He crossed the living room and picked up the phone.

"Yes?" he said.

"Let me talk to Amy." It was not a voice he recognized. A male voice, with a thick rural accent. It was the kind of voice that inspired immediate prejudice: the voice of an idiot; of a man without any right to make demands of him.

"Who is this?"

"Just let me talk to Amy."

"How about you go fuck yourself."

There was a pause as the man on the phone seemed to assess the obstacle. Then he said, with a trace of amusement in his voice, "Are you Brian?"

"That's right."

"Look, dude. Go get your wife. Put her on the phone. Do it now, and I won't have to come down there and break your fucking face."

Brian slammed down the receiver. Feeling suddenly light-headed, he put his hand on the wall to steady himself, to reassure himself that it was still solid, and that he was still real. From somewhere outside, through an open window, came the distant sound of children shouting.

It was obvious that Amy was sleeping with another man. When confronted with the call, she did not admit to anything, but made no special effort to explain it away, either. His name was Tommy, she said. She'd met him once when she was out. He sounded rough, but he wasn't a bad guy. She chose not to elaborate, and Brian, to his amazement, found a kind of forlorn comfort in his wife's affair. He'd lost his son; why not lose it all?

On television the news was filling with the creatures, more of which were being discovered all the time. The press had taken to calling them angels. Some were being found alive, though all of them appeared to have suffered from some violent experience. At least one family had become notorious by refusing to let anyone see the angel they'd found, or even let it out of their home. They boarded their windows and warned away visitors with a shotgun.

Brian was stationed on the couch, staring at the television with the sound turned down to barely a murmur. He listened to the familiar muted clatter from the medicine cabinet as Amy applied her makeup in the bathroom. A news program was on, and a handheld camera followed a street reporter into someone's house. The JD bottle was empty at his feet, and the knowledge that he had no more in the house smoldered in him.

Amy emerged from the kitchen with her purse slung over her arm and made her way to the door. "I'm going out," she said.

"Where?"

She paused, one hand on the doorknob. She wavered there, in her careful makeup and her push-up bra. He tried to remember the last time he'd seen her look like this and failed dismally. Something inside her seemed to collapse—a force of will, perhaps, or a habit of deception. Maybe she was just too tired to invent another lie.

"I'm going to see Tommy," she said.

"The redneck."

"Sure. The redneck, if that's how you want it."

"Does it matter how I want it?"

She paused. "No," she said. "I guess not."

"Well well. The truth. Look out."

She left the door, walked into the living room. Brian felt a sudden trepidation; this is not what he imagined would happen. He wanted to get a few weak barbs in before she walked out, that was all. He did not actually want to talk.

She sat on the rocking chair across from the couch. Beside her, on the television, the camera focused on an obese man wearing overalls smiling triumphantly and holding aloft an angel's severed head.

Amy shut it off. "Do you want to know about him?" she said.

"Let's see. He's stupid and violent. He called my home and threatened me. He's sleeping with my wife. What else is there to know?"

She appraised him for a moment, weighing consequences. "There's a little more to know," she said. "For example, he's very kind to me. He thinks I'm beautiful." He must have made some sort of sound then, because she said, "I know it must be very hard for you to believe, but some men still find me attractive. And that's important to me, Brian. Can you understand that?"

He turned away from her, shielding his eyes with a hand, although without the TV on there was very little light in the room. Each breath was laced with pain.

"When I go to see him, he talks to me. Actually talks. I know he might not be very smart, according to your standards, but you'd be surprised how much he and I have to talk about. You'd be surprised how much more there is to life—to my life—than your car magazines, and your TV, and your bottles of booze."

"Stop it," he said.

"He's also a very considerate lover. He paces himself. For my sake. For me. Did you ever do that, Brian? In all the times we made love?"

He felt tears crawling down his face. Christ. When did that start?

"I can forget things when I sleep with him. I can forget about . . . I can forget about everything. He lets me do that."

"You cold bitch," he rasped.

"You passive little shit," she bit back, with a venom that surprised him. "You let it happen, do you know that? You let it all happen. Every awful thing."

She stood abruptly and walked out the door, slamming it behind her. The force of it rattled the windows. After a while—he had no idea how long—he picked up the remote and turned the TV back on. A girl pointed to moving clouds on a map.

Eventually Dodger came by and curled up at his feet. Brian slid off the couch and lay down beside him, hugging him close. Dodger smelled the way dogs do, musky and of the earth, and he sighed with the abiding patience of his kind.

Violence filled his dreams. In them he rent bodies, spilled blood, painted the walls using severed limbs as gruesome brushes. In them he went back to the park and ate the children while the teacher looked on. Once he awoke after these dreams with blood filling his mouth; he realized he had chewed his tongue during the night. It was raw and painful for days afterward. A rage was building inside him and he could not find an outlet for it. One night Amy told him she thought she was falling in love with Tommy. He only nodded stupidly and watched her walk out the door again. That same night he kicked Dodger out of the house. He just opened the door to the night and told him to go. When he wouldn't—trying instead to slink around his legs and go back inside—he planted his foot on the dog's chest and physically pushed him back outside, sliding him backwards on his butt. "*Go find him!*" he yelled. "*Go find him! Go and find him!*" He shut the door and listened to Dodger whimper and scratch at it for nearly an hour. At some point he gave up and Brian fell asleep. When he awoke it was raining. He opened the door and called for him. The rain swallowed his voice.

"Oh no," he said quietly, his voice a whimper. "Come back! I'm sorry! Please, I'm so sorry!"

When Dodger did eventually return, wet and miserable, Brian hugged him tight, buried his face in his fur, and wept for joy.

Brian liked to do his drinking alone. When he drank in public, especially at his old bar, people tried to talk to him. They saw his presence as an invitation to share sympathy, or a request for a friendly ear. It got to be too much. But tonight he made his way back there, endured the stares and the weird silence, took the beers sent his way, although he wanted none of it. What he wanted tonight was Fire Engine, and she didn't disappoint.

Everybody knew Fire Engine, of course; if she thought you didn't know her, she'd introduce herself to you mighty quick. One hand on your shoulder, the other on your thigh. Where her hands went after that depended on a quick negotiation. She was a redhead with an easy personality, and was popular with the regular clientele, including the ones that would never buy her services. She claimed to be twenty-eight but looked closer to forty. At some unfortunate juncture in her life she had contrived to lose most of her front teeth, either to decay or to someone's balled fist; either way common wisdom held she gave the best blowjob in downtown New Orleans.

Brian used to be amused by that kind of talk. Although he'd never had an interest in her he'd certainly enjoyed listening to her sales pitch; she'd become a sort of bar pet, and the unself-conscious way she went about her life was both endearing and appalling. Her lack of teeth was too perfect, and too ridiculous. Now, however, the information had acquired a new kind of value to him. He pressed his gaze onto her until she finally felt it and looked back. She smiled coquettishly, with gruesome effect. He told the bartender to send her a drink.

"You sure? She ain't gonna leave you alone all night."

"Fuck yeah, I'm sure."

All night didn't concern him. What concerned him were the next ten minutes, which was what he figured ten dollars would buy him. After the necessary negotiations and bullshit they left the bar together, trailing catcalls; she took his hand and led him around back, into the alley.

The smell of rotting garbage came at him like an attack, like a pillowcase thrown over his head. She steered him into the alley's dark mouth, with its grime-smeared pavement and furtive skittering sounds, and its dumpster so stuffed with straining garbage bags that it looked like some fearsome monster choking on its dinner. "Now you know I'm a lady," she said, "but sometimes you just got to make do with what's available."

That she could laugh at herself this way touched Brian, and he felt a wash of sympathy for her. He considered what it would be like to run away with her, to rescue her from the wet pull of her life; to save her from people like himself.

She unzipped his pants and pulled his dick out. "There we go, honey, that's what I'm talking about. Ain't you something."

After a couple of minutes she released him and stood up. He tucked himself back in and zipped his pants, afraid to make eye contact with her.

"Maybe you just had too much to drink," she said.

"Yeah."

"It ain't nothing."

"I know it isn't," he said harshly.

When she made no move to leave, he said, "Will you just get the fuck away from me? Please?"

Her voice lost its sympathy. "Honey, I still got to get paid."

He opened his wallet and fished out a ten dollar bill. She plucked it from his fingers and walked out of the alley, back toward the bar. "Don't get all bent out of shape about it," she called. "Shit happens, you know?"

He slid down the wall until his ass hit the ground. He brought his hand to his mouth and choked out a sob, his eyes squeezed shut. He banged his head once against the brick wall behind him and then thought better of it. Down here the stench was a steaming blanket, almost soothing in its awfulness. He felt like he deserved to be there, that it was right that he should sleep in shit and grime. He listened to the gentle ticking of the roaches in the dark. He wondered if Toby was in a place like this.

Something glinted further down the alley. He strained to see it. It was too bright to be merely a reflection.

It moved.

"Son of a," he said, and pushed himself to his feet.

It lay mostly hidden; it had pulled some stray garbage bags atop itself in an effort to remain concealed, but its dim luminescence worked against it. Brian loped over to it, wrenched the bags away; its clawed hands clutched at them and tore them open, spilling a clatter of beer and liquor bottles all over the ground. They caromed with hollow music through the alley, coming at last to silent rest, until all Brian could hear was the thin, high-pitched noise the creature made through the tiny O-shaped orifice he supposed passed for a mouth. Its eyes were black little stones. The creature—*angel*, he thought, *they're calling these things angels*—was tall and thin, abundantly male, and it shed a thin light that illuminated exactly nothing around it. *If you put some clothes on it*, Brian thought, *hide its face, give it some gloves, it might pass for a human.*

Exposed, it held up a long-fingered hand, as if to ward him off. It had clearly been hurt: its legs looked badly broken, and it breathed in short, shallow gasps. A dark bruise spread like a mold over the right side of its chest.

"Look at you, huh? You're all messed up." He felt a strange glee as he said this; he could not justify the feeling and quickly buried it. "Yeah, somebody worked you over pretty good."

It managed to roll onto its belly, and it scrabbled along the pavement in a pathetic attempt at escape. It loosed that thin, reedy cry. Calling for help? Begging for its life?

The sight of it trying to flee from him catalyzed some deep predatory impulse, and he pressed his foot onto the angel's ankle, holding it easily in place. "No you don't." He hooked the thing beneath its shoulders and lifted it from the ground; it was astonishingly light. It

mewled weakly at him. "Shut up, I'm trying to help you." He adjusted
it in his arms so that he held it like a lover, or a fainted woman. He
carried it back to his car, listening for the sound of the barroom door
opening behind him, of laughter or a challenge chasing him down the
sidewalk. But the door stayed shut. He walked in silence.


Amy was awake when he got home, silhouetted in the doorway. Brian
pulled the angel from the passenger seat, cradled it against his chest.
He watched her face alter subtly, watched as some dark hope crawled
across it like an insect, and he squashed it before it could do any real
harm.

"It's not him," he said. "It's something else."

She stood away from the door and let him come in.

Dodger, who had been dozing in the hallway, lurched to his feet
with a sliding and skittering of claws and growled fiercely at it, his lips
curled away from his teeth.

"Get away, you," Brian said. He eased past him, bearing his load
down the hall.

He laid it in Toby's bed. Together he and Amy stood over it,
watching as it stared back at them with dark flat eyes, its body twisting
away from them as if it could fold itself into another place altogether.
Its fingers plucked at the train-spangled bedsheets, wrapping them
around its nakedness. Amy leaned over and helped to tuck she sheets
around it.

"He's hurt," she said.

"I know. I guess a lot of them are found that way."

"Should we call somebody?"

"You want camera crews in here? Fuck no."

"Well. He's really hurt. We need to do something."

"Yeah. I don't know. We can at least clean him up I guess."

Amy sat on the mattress beside it; it stared at her with its expres-
sionless face. Brian couldn't tell if there were thoughts passing behind

those eyes, or just a series of brute reflex arcs. After a moment it reached out with one long dark fingernail and brushed her arm. She jumped as though shocked.

"Jesus! Be careful," said Brian.

"What if it's him?"

"What?" It took him a moment to understand her. "Oh my God. Amy. It's not him, okay? It's not him."

"But what if it is?"

"It's not. We've seen them on the news, okay? It's a, it's a thing."

"You shouldn't call it an 'it.'"

*"How do I know what the fuck to call it?"*

She touched her fingers to its cheek. It pressed its face into them, making some small sound.

"Why did you leave me?" she said. "You were everything I had."

Brian swooned beneath a tide of vertigo. Something was moving inside him, something too large to stay where it was. "It's an angel," he said. "Nothing more. Just an angel. It's probably going to die on us, since that's what they seem to do." He put his hand against the wall until the dizziness passed. It was replaced by a low, percolating anger. "Instead of thinking of it as Toby, why don't you ask it where Toby is? Why don't you make it explain to us why it happened?"

She looked at him. "It happened because you let it," she said.


Dodger asked to be let outside. Brian opened the door for him to let him run around the front yard. There was a leash law here, but Dodger was well known by the neighbors and generally tolerated. He walked out of the house with considerably less than his usual enthusiasm. He lifted his leg desultorily against a shrub, then walked down to the road and followed the sidewalk further into the neighborhood. He did not come back.

Over the next few days it put its hooks into them, and drew them in tight. They found it difficult to leave it alone. Its flesh seemed to pump out some kind of soporific, like an invisible spoor, and it was better than the booze—better than anything they'd previously known. Its pull seemed to grow stronger as the days passed. For Amy, especially. She stopped going out, and for all practical purposes moved into Toby's room with it. When Brian joined her in there, she seemed to barely tolerate his presence. If he sat beside it she watched him with naked trepidation, as though she feared he might damage it somehow.

It was not, he realized, an unfounded fear. Something inside him became turbulent in its presence, something he couldn't identify but which sparked flashes of violent thought, of the kind he had not had since just after Toby vanished. This feeling came in sharp relief to the easy lethargy the angel normally inspired, and he was reminded of a time when he was younger, sniffing heroin laced with cocaine. So he did not object to Amy's efforts at excluding him.

Finally, though, her vigilance slipped. He went into the bathroom and found her sleeping on the toilet, her robe hiked up around her waist, her head resting against the sink. He left her there and crept into the angel's room.

It was awake, and its eyes tracked him as he crossed the room and sat beside it on the bed. Its breath wheezed lightly as it drew air through its puckered mouth. Its body was still bruised and bent, though it did seem to be improving.

Brian touched its chest where the bruise seemed to be diminishing. *Why does it bruise?* he wondered. *Why does it bleed the same way I do? Shouldn't it be made of something better?* Also, it didn't have wings. Not even vestigial ones. Why were they called angels? Because of how they made people feel? It looked more like an alien than a divine being. *It has a cock, for Christ's sake. What's that all about? Do angels fuck?*

He leaned over it, so his face was inches away, almost touching its nose. He stared into its black, irisless eyes, searching for some sign of intelligence, some evidence of intent or emotion. From this distance he could smell its breath; he drew it into his own lungs, and it warmed him like a shot of whiskey. The angel lifted its head and pressed its face into his. Brian jerked back and felt something brush his elbow. He looked behind him and discovered the angel had an erection.

He lurched out of bed, tripping over himself as he rushed to the door, dashed through it and slammed it shut. His blood sang. It rose in him like the sea and filled him with tumultuous music. He dropped to his knees and vomited all over the carpet.


Later, he stepped into its doorway, watching Amy trace her hands down its face. Through the window he could see that night was gathering in little pockets outside, lifting itself toward the sky. At the sight of the angel his heart jumped in his chest as though it had come unmoored. "Amy, I have to talk to you," he said. He had some difficulty making his voice sound calm.

She didn't look at him. "I know it's not really him," she said. "Not really."

"No."

"But don't you think he is, kind of? In a way?"

"No."

She laid her head on the pillow beside it, staring into its face. Brian was left looking at the back of her head, the unwashed hair, tangled and brittle. He remembered cupping the back of her head in his hand, its weight and its warmth. He remembered her body.

"Amy. Where does he live?"

"Who."

"Tommy. Where does he live?"

She turned and looked at him, a little crease of worry on her brow. "Why do you want to know?"

"Just tell me. Please."

"Brian, don't."

He slammed his fist into the wall, startling himself. He screamed at her. "*Tell me where he lives! God damn it!*"

Tommy opened the door of his shotgun house, clad only in boxer shorts, and Brian greeted him with a blow to the face. Tommy staggered back into his house, due more to surprise than the force of the punch; his foot slipped on a throw rug and he crashed to the floor. The small house reverberated with the impact. Brian had a moment to take in Tommy's hard physique and imagine his wife's hands moving over it. He stepped forward and kicked him in the groin.

Tommy grunted and seemed to absorb it. He rolled over and pushed himself quickly to his feet. Tommy's fist swung at him and he had time to experience a quick flaring terror before his head exploded with pain. He found himself on his knees, staring at the dust collecting in the crevices of the hardwood floor. Somewhere in the background a television chattered urgently.

A kick to the ribs sent Brian down again. Tommy straddled him, grabbed a fistful of hair, and slammed Brian's face into the floor several times. Brian felt something in his face break and blood poured onto the floor. He wanted to cry, but it was impossible; he couldn't get enough air. *I'm going to die*, he thought. He felt himself hauled up and thrown against a wall. Darkness crowded his vision. The world started to slide away.

Someone was yelling at him. There was a face in front of him, skin peeled back from its teeth in a smile or a grimace of rage. It looked like something from hell.

He awoke to the feel of cold grass, cold night air. The right side of his face burned like a signal flare; his left eye refused to open. It hurt to breathe. He pushed himself to his elbows and spit blood from his mouth; it immediately filled again. Something wrong in there. He rolled onto his back and laid there for a while, waiting for the pain to subside to a tolerable level. The night was high and dark. At one point he felt sure that he was rising from the ground, that something up there was pulling him into its empty hollows.

Somehow he managed the drive home. He remembered nothing of it except occasional stabs of pain as opposing headlights washed across his windshield; he would later consider his safe arrival a kind of miracle. He pulled into the driveway and honked the horn a few times until Amy came out and found him there. She looked at him with horror, and with something else.

"Oh, baby. What did you do. What did you do."

She steered him toward the angel's room. He stopped himself in the doorway, his heart pounding again, and he tried to catch his breath. It occurred to him, on a dim level, that his nose was broken. She tugged at his hand, but he resisted. Her face was limned by moonlight, streaming through the window like some mystical tide, and by the faint luminescence of the angel tucked into their son's bed. She'd grown heavy over the years, and the past year had taken a harsh toll: the flesh on her face sagged, and was scored by grief. And yet he was stunned by her beauty.

Had she always looked like this?

"Come on," she said. "Please."

The left side of his face pulsed with hard beats of pain; it sang like a war drum. His working eye settled on the thing in the bed: its flat black eyes, its wickedly curved talons. Amy sat beside it and put her hand on its chest. It arched its back, seeming to coil beneath her.

"Come lay down," she said. "He's here for us. He's come home for us."

Brian took a step into Toby's room, and then another. He knew she was wrong; that the angel was not home, that it had wandered here from somewhere far away.

*Is heaven a dark place?*

The angel extended a hand, its talons flexing. The sheets over its belly stirred as Brian drew closer. Amy took her husband's hands, easing him onto the bed. He gripped her shoulders, squeezing them too tightly. "I'm sorry," he said suddenly, surprising himself. "I'm sorry! I'm sorry!" Once he began he couldn't stop. He said it over and over again, so many times it just became a sound, a sobbing plaint, and Amy pressed her hand against his mouth, entwined her fingers into his hair, saying, "Shhhh, shhhhh," and finally she silenced him with a kiss. As they embraced each other the angel played its hands over their faces and their shoulders, its strange reedy breath and its narcotic musk drawing them down to it. They caressed each other, and they caressed the angel, and when they touched their lips to its skin the taste of it shot spikes of joy through their bodies. Brian felt her teeth on his neck and he bit into the angel, the sudden dark spurt of blood filling his mouth, the soft pale flesh tearing easily, sliding down his throat. He kissed his wife furiously and when she tasted the blood she nearly tore his tongue out; he pushed her face toward the angel's body, and watched the blood blossom from beneath her. The angel's eyes were frozen, staring at the ceiling; it extended a shaking hand toward a wall decorated with a Spider-Man poster, its fingers twisted and bent.

They ate until they were full.

That night, heavy with the sludge of bliss, Brian and Amy made love again for the first time in nearly a year. It was wordless and slow, a synchronicity of pressures and tender familiarities. They were like rare creatures of a dying species, amazed by the sight of each other.

Brian drifts in and out of sleep. He has what will be the last dream about his son. It is morning in this dream, by the side of a small country road. It must have rained during the night, because the world shines with a wet glow. Droplets of water cling, dazzling, to the muzzle of a dog as it rests beside the road, unmenaced by traffic, languorous and dull-witted in the rising heat. It might even be Dodger. His snout is heavy with blood. Some distance away from him Toby rests on the street, a small pile of bones and torn flesh, glittering with dew, catching and throwing sunlight like a scattered pile of rubies and diamonds.

By the time he wakes, he has already forgotten it.

# Sunbleached

*"We're God's beautiful creatures,"* the vampire said, something like joy leaking into its voice for the first time since it had crawled under this house four days ago. "We're the pinnacle of his art. If you believe in that kind of thing, anyway. That's why the night is our time. He hangs jewels in the sky for us. People, they think we're at some kinda disadvantage because we can't go out in the sunlight. But who needs it. The day is small and cramped. You got your one lousy star."

"You believe in God?" Joshua asked. The crawlspace beneath his house was close and hot; his body was coated in a dense sheen of sweat. A cockroach crawled over his fingers and he jerked his hand away. Late summer pressed onto this small Mississippi coastal town like the heel of a boot. The heat was an act of violence.

"I was raised Baptist. My thoughts on the matter are complicated."

The crawlspace was contained partially by sheets of aluminum siding and partially by decaying wooden latticework. It was by this latter that Joshua crouched, hiding in the hot spears of sunlight which intruded into the shadows and made a protective cage around him.

"That's why it's so easy for us to seduce. God loves us, so the world does, too. Seduction is your weapon, kid. You're what—fifteen?

You think seduction is pumping like a jackrabbit in your momma's car. You don't know anything. But you will soon enough."

The vampire moved in the shadows, and abruptly the stink of burnt flesh and spoiled meat greased the air. It had opened a wound in itself by moving. Joshua knew that it tried to stay still as much as it could, to facilitate the healing, but the slowly shifting angles of the sunbeams made that impossible. He squinted his eyes, trying to make out a shape, but it was useless. He could sense it back there, though— a dark, fluttering presence. Something made of wings.

"Invite me in," it said.

"Later," Joshua said. "Not yet. After you finish changing me."

The vampire coughed; it sounded like a snapping bone. Something wet hit the ground. "Well come here then, boy." It moved again, this time closer to the amber light. Its face emerged from the shadows like something rising from deep water. It hunched on its hands and knees, swinging its head like a dog trying to catch a scent. Its face had been burnt off. Thin, parchment-strips of skin hung from blackened sinew and muscle. Its eyes were dark, hollow caves. Even in this wretched state, though, it seemed weirdly graceful. A dancer pretending to be a spider.

For the second time, Joshua laid himself on the soft earth, a-crawl with ants and cockroaches, centipedes and earthworms, positioning his upper body beyond the reach of the streaming sunlight. The light's color was deepening, its angles rising until they were almost parallel to the ground. Evening was settling over the earth.

The vampire pressed the long fingers of one charred hand onto his chest, as delicately as a lover. Heat flushed Joshua's body. Every nerve ending was a trembling candle flame. The vampire touched its lips to his throat; its tongue sought the jugular, the heavy river inside. It slid its teeth into his skin.

A sharp, lovely pain.

Joshua stared at the underside of his home: the rusted pipes, the duct tape, the yellow sheets of insulation. It looked so different from beneath. So ugly. He heard footsteps overhead as somebody he loved moved around inside it, attending to mysterious offices.


Four days ago: he'd stood on the front porch of his home in the deep blue hollow of early morning, watching the waters of the Gulf roll onto the beach. It was his favorite time of the day: that sweet, lonesome hinge between darkness and daylight, when he could pretend he was alone in the world and free to take it on his own terms. In a few moments he would go inside and wake his five-year-old brother, Michael, make him breakfast, and get them both ready for school, while their mother still slept in after her night shift at Red Lobster.

But this time belonged to him.

The vampire came from the direction of town, trailing black smoke and running hard across the no-man's land between his own house and the nearest standing building. There'd been a neighborhood there once, but the hurricane wiped it away a few years ago. What remained had looked like a mouthful of shattered teeth, until the state government came through and razed everything to the ground. Their own house had been badly damaged—the storm had scalped it of its top floor, depositing it somewhere out in the Gulf—but the rest had stood its ground, though it canted steeply to one side now, and on windy days you could feel it coming through the walls.

It was over that empty expanse the vampire fled, first billowing smoke like a diesel engine and then erupting into flame as the sun cracked the horizon.

The vampire ran directly for his house and launched itself at the opening to the crawlspace under the porch steps. Oily smoke eeled up through the wooden planks and dissipated into the lightening sky.

Joshua had remained frozen in place for the whole event, save the rising clamor in his heart.

*℘♥*

Their mother would be late getting home from work—and even later if she went out with that jackass Tyler again—so Joshua fed his little brother and directed him to his bedroom. They passed the stairwell on their way, which was capped now by sheets of plywood hammered over the place where it used to open onto the second floor.

"You want me to read you a story?" he asked, reaching for the copy of *The Wind in the Willows* by the bedside. Michael didn't really understand the story, but he liked it when Joshua did the voices.

"No," he said, leaping into his bed and pulling the covers over himself.

"No story? Are you sure?"

"I just wanna go to sleep tonight."

"Okay," Joshua said. He felt strangely bereft. He reached down and turned on Michael's nightlight, then switched off the lamp.

"Will you cuddle with me, Josh?" he said.

"I won't 'cuddle' with you, but I'll lay down with you for a little bit."

"Okay."

Cuddle was a word their dad used before he moved away, and it embarrassed him that Michael held onto it. He eased back on top of the covers and let Michael rest his head in the crook of his arm.

"Are you scared of anything, Josh?"

"What, like monsters?"

"I don't know, I guess."

"No, I'm not scared of monsters. I'm not scared of anything."

Michael thought for a minute, then said, "I'm scared of storms."

"That's silly. It's just a bunch of wind and rain."

". . . I know."

Michael drifted into silence. Joshua felt vaguely guilty about shutting him down like that, but he really didn't have it in him to have the storm talk again. That was something Michael was going to have to get over on his own, since logic didn't seem to have any effect on his thinking.

As he monitored his brother's breathing, waiting for him to fall asleep, he found himself wondering about how he would feel toward his family once the transformation was complete. He was worried that he would lose all feeling for them. Or, worse, that he'd think of them as prey. He didn't think that would happen; most things he'd ever read about vampires seemed to indicate that they kept all their memories and emotions from life. But the thought troubled him nonetheless.

That was why he wouldn't let the vampire into his house until he became one, too; he wanted to be sure it went after the right person. It couldn't have his family.

The question of love was tricky, anyway. He felt protective of his brother and his mom, but he had a hard time aligning that feeling with a word like love. Maybe it was the same thing; he honestly didn't know. He tried to imagine how he'd feel if they were gone, and he didn't come up with much.

That thought troubled him even more.

Maybe he would think of Michael and his mother as pets. The notion brightened his mood.

People loved their pets.

Michael pretended to be asleep until Joshua left the room. He loved his older brother in the strong, uncomplicated way children loved anything; but recently he'd become an expert in negotiating the emotional weather in his home, and Joshua's moods had become more turbulent than ever. He got mad at strange things, like when Michael wanted to hold hands, or when Mom brought Tyler home. Michael thought Tyler was weird because he wouldn't talk to them, but he didn't understand why Joshua got so mad about it.

He listened as his brother's footsteps receded down the hallway. He waited a few more minutes just to be sure. Then he slid down and scooted under the bed on his stomach, pressing his ear to the floor. The house swayed and creaked around him, filling the night with bizarre noises. He hated living here since the storm happened. He felt like he was living in the stomach of a monster.

After a few minutes of careful listening, he heard the voice.


Joshua opened his window and waited. He didn't even try to sleep anymore, even though he was constantly tired. The night was clear and cool, with a soft breeze coming in from the sea. The palm trees across the street rustled quietly to themselves, shaggy-haired giants sharing secrets.

After about half an hour, the vampire crawled from an opening near the back of the house, emerging just a few feet from his window. Joshua's heart started to gallop. He felt the familiar, instinctive fear: the reaction of the herd animal to the lion.

The vampire stood upright, facing the sea. Most of its flesh had burnt away; the white round curve of its skull reflected moonlight. Its clothes were dark rags in the wind.

A car pulled into the driveway around front, its engine idling for a few moments before chuckling to a halt. Mom was home.

The vampire's body seemed to coil, every muscle drawing taut at once. It lifted its nose, making tiny jerking motions, looking for the scent.

He heard his mother's laughter, and a man's voice. Tyler was with her.

The vampire took a step toward the front of the house, its joints too loose, as if they were hinged with liquid instead of bone and ligament. Even in its broken, half-dead state, it moved quickly and fluidly. He thought again of a dancer. He imagined how it would look in full health, letting the night fill its body like a kite. Moving through the air like an eel through water.

"Take him," Joshua whispered.

The vampire turned its eyeless face toward him.

Joshua was smiling. "Take him," he said again.

"You know I can't," it said, rage riding high in its voice. "Why the hell don't you let me in!"

"That's not the deal," he said. "Afterwards. Then you can come in. And you can have Tyler."

He heard the front door open, and the voices moved inside. Mom and Tyler were in the living room, giggling and whispering. Half drunk already.

"He's all I'll need," the vampire said. "Big country boy like that. Do me right up."

Someone knocked on his bedroom door. His mother's voice came through. "Josh? Are you on the phone in there? You're supposed to be asleep!"

"Sorry, Mom," he said over his shoulder. He heard Tyler's muffled voice, and his mother started laughing. "Shhh!" It made Joshua's stomach turn. When he looked back outside, the vampire had already slid back under the house.

He sighed and leaned his head out, feeling the cool wind on his face. The night was vast above him. He imagined rising into it, through clouds piled like snowdrifts and into a wash of ice crystal stars, waiting for its boundary but not finding one. Just rising higher and higher into the dark and the cold.

The school day passed in a long, punishing haze. His ability to concentrate was fading steadily. His body felt like it was made of lead. He'd never been so exhausted in his life, but every time he closed his eyes he was overcome with a manic energy, making him fidget in his chair. It took the whole force of his will not to get up and start pacing the classroom.

A fever simmered in his brain. He touched the back of his hand to his forehead and was astonished by the heat. Sounds splintered in his ear, and the light coming through the windows was sharp-edged. His gaze roved over the classroom, over his classmates hunched over their desks or whispering carelessly in the back rows or staring like farm animals into the empty air. He'd never been one of them, and that was okay. It was just how things were. He used to feel smaller than them, less significant, as if he'd been born without some essential gene to make him acceptable to other people.

But now he assessed them anew. They seemed different, suddenly. They looked like victims. Like little pink pigs, waiting for someone to slash their throats and fulfill their potential. He imagined the room bathed in blood, himself striding through it, a raven amongst the carcasses. Strutting like any carrion king.

He was halfway into the crawlspace when nausea overwhelmed him and he dry heaved into the dirt, the muscles in his sides seizing in pain. He curled into a fetal position and pressed his face into the cool earth until it subsided, leaving him gasping in exhaustion. His throat was swollen and dry.

"I can't sleep," the vampire said from the shadows.

Joshua blinked and lifted his gaze, still not raising his head from the ground. He didn't think he could summon the strength for it, even if he'd wanted to.

The vampire was somewhere in the far corner beneath the house, somewhere behind the bars of sunlight slanting through the latticework. "The light moves around too much down here," it said, apparently oblivious to Joshua's pain. "I can't rest. I need to rest."

Joshua was silent. He didn't know what he was expected to say.

"Invite me in," it said. "I can make it dark inside."

"What's happening to me?" Joshua asked. He had to force the air out of his lungs to speak. He could barely hear himself.

"You're changing. You're almost there."

"I feel like I'm dying."

"Heh, that's funny."

Joshua turned his face into the soil. He felt a small tickling movement crawling up his pant leg.

"I remember when I died. I was terrified. It's okay to be scared, Joshua."

That seemed like a funny thing to say. He blinked, staring into the place where the voice was coming from.

"I was in this barn. I was a hand on this farm that grew sugar cane. Me and a few others slept out there in the loft. One day this young fella turned up missing. We didn't think too much about it. Good-natured boy, worked hard, but he was kinda touched in the head, and we figured it was always a matter of time before he went and got himself into some trouble. We thought we'd wait for the weekend and then go off and look for him.

"But he came back before the weekend. Sailed in through the second-floor window of the barn one night. I about pissed myself. Seemed like he walked in on a cloud. Before we could think of anything to say, he laid into us. Butchered most of the boys like hogs. Three of us he left, though. Maybe 'cause we were nicer to him, I don't know. He decided to make us like him. Who knows why. But see, he was too stupid to tell us what was going on. Didn't know himself, I guess. But he just kept us up there night after night, feeding on us a little bit at a time. Our dead friends around us the whole time, growing flies."

"Why didn't you run when the sun came up?" Joshua had forgotten his pain. He sat up, edging closer to the ribbons of light, his head hunched below the underside of the house.

"Son of a bitch spiked our legs to the floor of the loft. Wrapped barbed wire around our arms. He was determined, I'll give him that. And no one came from the house. Didn't take a genius to figure out why." The vampire paused, seemingly lost in the memory. "Well anyway, before too long we got up and started our new lives. He went off God knows where. So did the other two. Never seen them since."

Joshua took it all in, feeling the shakes come on again. "I'm worried about my family," he said. "I'm worried they won't understand."

"You won't feel so sentimental, afterwards."

This was too much to process. He decided he needed to sleep for a while. Let the fever abate, then approach it all with a fresh mind.

"I'm gonna lay down," he said, turning back toward the opening. The light there was like a boiling cauldron, but the thought of lying in his own bed was enough to push through.

"Wait!" the vampire said. "I need to feed first."

Joshua decided to ignore it. He was already crawling out, and he didn't have the energy to turn around.

"BOY!"

He froze, and looked behind him. The vampire lunged forward, and its head passed into a sunbeam. The flesh hissed, emitting a thin coil of smoke. A candle flame flared around it, and the stench of ruined flesh rolled over him in a wave, as though a bag of rancid meat had been torn open.

The vampire pulled back, the blind sockets of his eyes seeming to float in the dim white bone. "Don't play with me, boy."

"I'm not," Joshua said. "I'll be back later." And he crawled out into the jagged sunlight.


He awoke to find his mother hovering over him. She was wearing her white Red Lobster shirt, with the nametag and the ridiculous tie. She had one hand on his forehead, simultaneously taking his temperature and pushing the hair out of his face.

"Hey, honey," she said.

"Mom?" He pulled his head away from her and passed a hand over his face. He was on the couch in the living room. Late afternoon light streamed in through the window. No more than an hour could have elapsed. "What are you doing home?"

"Mikey called me. He said you passed out."

He noticed his brother sitting on the easy chair on the other side of the room. Michael regarded him solemnly, his little hands folded in his lap like he was in church.

"You're white as a sheet," his mother said. "How long have you been feeling bad?"

"I don't know. Just today, I guess."

"I think we should get you to a hospital."

"No!" He made an effort to sit up. "No, I'm fine. I just need to rest for a while."

She straightened, and he could see her wrestling with the idea. He knew she didn't want to go to the hospital any more than he did. They didn't have any insurance, and here she was missing a shift at work besides.

"Really, I'm okay. Besides, we'd have to wait forever, and isn't Tyler coming over tonight?"

His mother tensed. She looked at him searchingly, like she was trying the fathom his motive. She said, "Joshua, you're more important to me than Tyler is. You do understand that, don't you?"

He looked away. He felt his face flush, and he didn't want her to see it. "I know," he said.

"I know you don't like him."

"It's not that," he said, but of course it was that. Tyler had to be here so he could feed him to the vampire. He had a feeling that tonight was going to be the night. He didn't know how he could go on much more, as weak as he was.

Michael piped up, his voice cautious yet hopeful: "It doesn't matter anyway, 'cause Daddy's coming back."

His mother sighed and turned to look at him. Joshua could see all the years gathered in her face, and he felt a sudden and unexpected sympathy for her. "No, Mikey. He's not."

"Yes he is, Mom, he told me. He asked if it was okay."

Her voice hardened, although she was obviously trying to hide it. "Has he been talking to you on the phone?" She looked to Joshua for confirmation.

"Not me," Joshua said. It occurred to him that Dad may have been calling while he was under the house, talking to the vampire. He felt at once both guilty that he'd left his brother to deal with that alone, and outraged that he'd missed out on the calls.

"You tell him next time he calls that he can talk to me about that," she said, not even bothering to hide her anger now. "In fact, don't even talk to him. Hang up on him if he calls again. I'm going to get his number blocked, that son of a bitch."

Tears gathered in Michael's eyes, and he lowered his face. His body trembled as he tried to keep it all inside. A wild anger coursed through Joshua's body, animating him despite the fever.

"Shut up!" he shouted. "Shut up about Dad! You think Tyler is better? He can't even look at us! He's a fucking *retard!*"

His mother looked at him in pained astonishment for a long moment. Then she put her hand over her mouth and stifled a sob. Aghast, Michael launched himself at her, a terrified little missile. He wrapped his arms around her and buried his face in her chest. "It's okay, Mom, it's okay!"

Joshua unfolded himself from the couch and walked down the hall to his room. His face was alight with shame and rage. He didn't know what to do. He didn't know what to feel. He closed the door behind him, muffling the sounds of the others comforting each other. He threw himself onto his bed, pulling the pillow over his face. The only things he could hear now were the wooden groaning of the house as it shifted on its foundations, and the diminished sound of the blood pumping in his own head.

Their father left right after the hurricane. He used to work on the oil rigs. He'd get on a helicopter and disappear for a few weeks, and money would show up in the bank account. Then he'd come home for a week, and they'd all have fun together. He'd fight with their mother sometimes, but he always went back out to sea before things had a chance to get bad.

After the hurricane, all that work dried up. The rigs were compromised and the Gulf Coast oil industry knocked back on its heels. Dad was stranded in the house. Suddenly there was no work to stop the fighting. He moved to California shortly thereafter, saying he'd send for them when he found another job. A week later their mother told them the truth.

Joshua still remembered the night of the storm. The four of them rode it out together in the house. It sounded like Hell itself had come unchained and was stalking the world right outside their window. But he felt safe inside. Even when the upper floor ripped away in a scream of metal and plaster and wood, revealing a black, twisting sky, he never felt like he was in any real danger. The unremarkable sky he'd always known had changed into something three-dimensional and alive.

It was like watching the world break open, exposing its secret heart.

His father was crouched beside him. They stared at it together in amazement, grinning like a pair of blissed-out lunatics.

Joshua heard a gentle rapping on his door.

"I'm going to the store," his mother said. "I'm gonna get something for your fever. Is there anything you want for dinner?"

"I'm not hungry."

He waited for her car to pull out of the driveway before he swung his legs out of bed and tried to stand. He could do it as long as he kept one hand on the wall. He couldn't believe how tired he was. His whole body felt cold, and he couldn't feel his fingers. It was coming tonight. The certainty of it inspired no excitement, no joy, no fear. His body was too numb to feel anything. He just wanted it to happen so he could get past this miserable stage.

He shuffled out of his room and down the hall. The vampire needed to feed on him once more, and he wanted to get down there before his mother got back.

As he passed by his brother's door, though, he stopped short. Somebody was whispering on the other side.

He opened the door to find his little brother lying prone on the floor, half under the bed. Late afternoon shadows gathered in the corners. His face was a small moon in the dim light, one ear pressed to the hardwood. He was whispering urgently.

"Michael?"

His brother's body jerked in alarm, and he sat up quickly, staring guiltily back. Joshua flipped the light switch on.

"What are you doing?" Something cold was growing inside him. Michael shrugged.

"Tell me!"

"Talking to Daddy."

"No."

"He's living under the house. He wants us to let him back in. I was afraid to because Mom might get mad at me."

". . . oh, Mikey." His voice quavered. "That's not Dad. That's not Dad."

He found himself moving down the hall again, quickly now, fired with renewed energy. He felt like a passenger in his body: he experienced a mild curiosity as he saw himself rummaging through the kitchen drawer until he found the claw hammer his mother kept there; a sense of fearful anticipation as he pushed the front door open and stumbled down the porch steps in the failing light, not even pausing to gather his strength before he hooked the claw into the nearest latticework and wrenched it away from the wall in a long segment.

"We had a deal!" he screamed, getting to work on another segment. "You son of a bitch! We had a deal!" He worked fast, alternately smashing wooden latticework to pieces and prying aluminum panels free from the house. "You lied to me! You lied!" Nails squealed as they were wrenched from their moorings. The sun was too low for the light to intrude beneath the house now, but tomorrow the vampire would find the crawlspace uninhabitable.

He saw the vampire, once, just beneath the lip of the house. It said nothing, but its face tracked him as he worked.

The sun was sliding down the sky, leaking its light into the ground and into the sea. Darkness swarmed from the east, spreading stars in its wake.

Joshua hurried inside, dropping the hammer on the floor and collapsing onto the couch, utterly spent. A feeling of profound loss hovered somewhere on the edge of his awareness. He had turned his back on something, on some grand possibility. He knew the pain would come later.

Soon his mother returned, and he took some of the medicine she'd bought for him, though he didn't expect it to do any good. He made a cursory attempt to eat some of the pizza she'd brought, too, but his appetite was gone. She sat beside him on the couch and brushed the hair away from his forehead. They watched some TV, and Joshua slipped in and out of sleep. At one point he stared through the window over the couch. The moon traced a glittering arc through the sky. Constellations rotated above him and the planets rolled through the heavens. He felt a yearning that nearly pulled him out of his body.

He could see for billions of miles.

At some point his mother roused him from the couch and guided him to his room. He cast a glance into Michael's room when he passed it, and saw his brother fast asleep.

"You know I love you, Josh," his mother said at his door.

He nodded. "I know, Mom. I love you, too."

His body was in agony. He was pretty sure he was going to die, but he was too tired to care.

A scream woke him. The heavy sound of running footsteps, followed by a crash.

Then silence.

Joshua tried to rouse himself. He felt like he'd lost control of his body. His eyelids fluttered open. He saw his brother standing in the doorway, tears streaming down his face.

"Oh no, Josh, oh no, oh no . . ."

He lost consciousness.


The next morning he was able to move again. The fever had broken sometime during the night; his sheets were soaked with sweat.

He found his mother on the kitchen table. She had kicked some plates and silverware onto the floor in what had apparently been a brief struggle. Her head was hanging backward off the edge of the table, and she had been sloppily drained. Blood splashed the floor beneath her. Her eyes were open and glassy.

His brother was suspended upside down in the living room, his feet tied with a belt to the ceiling fan, which had come partially free from its anchor. He'd been drained, too. He was still wearing his pajamas. On the floor a few feet away from him, where it had fluttered to rest, was a welcome home card he had made for their father.

The plywood covering the open stairwell had been wrenched free. The vampire stood on the top stair, looking into the deep blue sky of early morning. Joshua stopped at the bottom stair, gazing up at it. Its burnt skin was covered in a clear coating of pus and lymphatic fluid, as its body started to heal. White masses filled its eye sockets like spiders' eggs. Tufts of black hair stubbled its peeled head.

"I waited for you," the vampire said.

Joshua's lower lip trembled. He tried to say something, but he couldn't get his voice to work.

The vampire extended a hand. "Come up here. The sun's almost up."

Almost against his will, he ascended the stairs into the open air. The vampire wrapped its fingers around the back of his head and drew him close. Its lips grazed his neck. It touched its tongue to his skin.

"Thank you for your family," it said.

". . . no . . ."

It sank its teeth into Joshua's neck and drew from him one more time. A gorgeous heat seeped through his body, and he found himself being lowered gently to the top of the stair.

"It's okay to be afraid," the vampire said.

His head rolled to one side; he looked over the area where the second story used to be. There was his old room. There was Michael's. And that's where his parents slept. Now it was all just open air.

"This is my house now," the vampire said, standing over him and surveying the land around them. "At least for a few more days." It looked down at Joshua with its pale new eyes. "I'd appreciate it if you stayed out."

The vampire descended the stairs.

A few minutes later, the sun came up, first as a pink stain, then as a gash of light on the edge of the world. Joshua felt the heat rising in him again: a fierce, purging radiance starting from his belly and working rapidly outward. He smelled himself cooking, watched the smoke begin to pour out of him, crawling skyward.

And then the day swung its heavy lid over the sky. The ground baked hard as an anvil in the heat, and the sun hammered the color out of everything.

# North American Lake Monsters

*Grady and Sarah shuffled out of the cabin,* bundled in heavy jackets and clutching mugs of coffee that threw heat like dark little suns. Across the wide expanse of Tipton's Lake the Blue Ridge Mountains breached the morning fog banks, their tree-lined backs resembling the foresty spines of some great kraken trawling the seas. Together they descended the steps from the front porch onto the unkempt grass and made their way down to the lake's edge, and onto the small path which would lead them a couple hundred feet along until they came to the body of the strange creature that had washed ashore and died there.

They did not speak much as they walked. Out of jail for only three days after six years inside, Grady was struggling to recognize his thirteen-year-old daughter in the sullen-eyed, cynical presence striding along beside him. She had undergone some bizarre transformation since he'd last seen her. She'd dyed her hair black; strange silver adornments pocked her face: she had a ring in her left eyebrow, and a series of rings along the curve of one bejeweled conch of an ear. Worst of all, she'd put a stud through her tongue.

"Man, I can really smell that thing," he said. Sarah had discovered it last night, and was eager to show it off. The early cold snap had held off the smell to some degree, but it was beginning to creep toward the cabin.

"Wait till you see it, Dad, it's amazing."

Sarah had not come to see him during his last three years in prison. At first that had been at his own insistence, and she'd taken it badly: he told her of his decision while she and her mother were visiting, and she threw a tantrum of such violence that the guards were obliged to cut their session short. His reasons, he thought, were both predictable and justified: he didn't want his little girl to see him in that environment, slowly eroding into a smaller, meaner, beaten man. But the truth was simply that he was ashamed, and by keeping his daughter away he spared himself the humiliation he felt in her company. After less than a year of that, though, his resolve failed, and he asked his wife to start bringing her again. But Sarah never came back.

They rounded a thick copse of pines, cutting off their view of the cabin. From this vantage point it was easy to imagine themselves far from civilization and all its attendant rules. Cold air blew in off the lake. Grady lowered his chin into his jacket and closed his eyes, smelling the pine, the soft wet stink of the mud, the aroma of real coffee. He'd smelled nothing but sweat, urine, and disinfectant for so long that it seemed to him now that he was walking through the foothills of Heaven.

"I don't know what you think you're gonna do with it," Sarah said, ranging ahead. She cradled the mug of coffee he'd made for her like a kitten against her chest. "It's way too big to move."

"Won't know till I see it," he said.

"I was just telling you," she said, sounding hurt.

Grady was immediately irritated. "I didn't mean it like that." Christ, managing her moods was like handling nitroglycerin. Wasn't she supposed to be tough, with all that shit on her face? The old anger—irrational and narcotic in its sweetness—stirred in him. "So who's this boy your mother told me about? What's his name . . . Tracy?"

"Travis," she said, her voice muted.

"Oh. *Travis.*"

She said nothing, picking up her pace a little bit. She was on the defensive, which only provoked him. He wanted her to fight. "What grade is he in?"

Again, nothing.

"Does he even go to school?"

"Yes," she said, but he could barely hear her.

"He better not be in fucking high school."

She turned on him; he noticed, with some dismay, that she had tears in her eyes. "I know Mom already told you all about him! Why are you doing this?"

"*Jesus*, what are you crying about? Never mind what your mom told me, I want to hear this from you."

"He's in ninth grade, all right? You should be glad I'm dating an older boy, he's not an immature shithead like the boys in my school!" Grady just stood there, trying to decide how to feel. He felt a calmness descend over him, in an inverse proportion to Sarah's distress. He studied her. Did she really believe what she was saying? Had she grown so stupid in his absence?

"Well. I guess I ought to be grateful. Do I get to meet this Travis when we get back to Winston-Salem?"

She turned and continued down the path.

After a few more moments of trudging in strained silence, they rounded a small bend and came upon the monster. It was as big as a small van, still partly submerged in the lake, as though it had lunged onto the ground and expired from the effort. Grady drifted to a halt without realizing it, and Sarah went ahead without him, walking up to the huge carcass as casually as if she were approaching a boulder or a wrecked ship.

"Jesus, Sarah, don't touch it."

She ignored him and pressed her fingertips against its hide. "What are you afraid of? It's dead."

He was having trouble apprehending its shape. It looked like a huge, suppurated heart. It seemed a confusion of forms, as though the weight of the atmosphere crushed it out of true: he had the strong impression that underwater it would unfurl into something sensible, though perhaps no less strange. Its skin, glistening with dew and sickly excretions, was dark green, almost black. Enfolded in the flesh near the mud was an eye: saucer-sized, clouded, eclipsed by a nictitating membrane which covered it like a bone-white crescent moon. A two-foot-long gash was partially buried in the mud; it could have been a mouth, or the wound that killed it. An odor seeped from it like a gas, candy-sweet.

Grady felt his stomach buckle. "What . . . what is it?"

"I don't know," Sarah said. "It's a dinosaur or something."

"Don't be stupid."

She went silent, pacing calmly around it.

"We need to uh . . . we need to get rid of it. Push it in or something." The thought of this smell rolling into the cabin windows at night fueled an irrational rage inside him. It wasn't right that this atrocity should ruin his homecoming.

"You can't. I already tried."

"Yeah, well. Maybe I'll try again." He placed his hands on it with great reluctance and gave it a cursory push to get a sense of its weight. The flesh gave a bit, and he felt his hands sink. He wrenched them away, making a high-pitched sound he didn't recognize as his own. His hands were covered in a sticky film, as though he'd gripped a sappy tree. Nausea swelled in his body; the ground swung up to meet him and he vomited into the mud.

"Oh my God. Dad?"

He continued to dry heave until it felt like his guts were crawling up his throat. He smelled coffee on the ground in front of him, and he crawled away from it. "Oh Jesus, oh Jesus."

Sarah pulled at his shoulders. "Dad? Are you okay?"

He managed to lean back into a sitting position, rubbing his hands hard against his pants, trying to wipe off the sticky residue. He thought that if he moved it would trigger another spasm, so he sat still for a few moments and gathered himself. He could hear his daughter's voice. It seemed to come from an immeasurable distance. He crawled over to the water and thrust his hands into it, trying to scrape the residue from his hands without success.

The thing would have to be destroyed. Maybe if he hacked it up he could push it back into the lake. They were staying at his father-in-law's cabin; surely the man kept a chainsaw or an axe around for chopping wood.

Eventually, he grabbed her arm, hauling himself to his feet. His mug lay near the monster, splashed in mud. He decided to leave it there.

"Let's go," he said. He started back along the path without waiting to see if she'd follow. He continued to scrape his hands on his thighs, but he was beginning to doubt the stuff would come off.

Tina was awake by the time they returned. She was leaning against the porch railing, one hand clutching her robe closed at her neck and the other holding a cigarette. Her eyes were heavy-lidded, her hair sleep-crushed, her hangover as heavy as a mantle of chains. She stood up there like a promise of life, and something stirred in Grady at the sight of her, grateful and tender. He summoned a smile from some resolute part of himself and raised a hand in greeting.

"You look like shit," she said amiably.

He looked down at himself. "I fell."

"So did you see it?"

"Oh yeah, I saw it."

"Mom, he got sick!"

He closed his eyes. "Sarah . . ."

"You got sick, baby?"

"Just, I—yeah, okay, I got sick. It's fucking disgusting."

They climbed the stairs and joined her on the porch. Tina brushed at his pants with one hand, her cigarette clenched in her teeth. "Sarah, go get a towel from the bathroom. You can't walk into the cabin like this."

"It's all over my hands," Grady said.

"What is?"

"I don't know, some weird sticky shit on the, on the thing. I think it gave me a reaction or something."

"We should get you to a doctor, Dad," said Sarah.

"Don't be stupid. I just got a little dizzy."

"Dad, you—"

"Goddamnit, Sarah!"

She stepped back from him as though she'd been struck. Tina gestured at her without looking, still brushing her husband's pants. "Sarah—honey—a towel. Please."

Sarah's mouth moved silently for a moment; then she said, "Fine," and went inside. Grady watched her go, fighting down a spike of anger.

"What's your problem?" said Tina, giving up on his pants.

"*My* problem? Is that a joke?"

"You been gone six years, Grady. Give her a chance."

"Well, it was her choice not to see me for the last three of them. I didn't ask her to stay away. Not at the end. And anyway, is that what you're doing? Giving her a chance? Is that what the rings in her face and that shit in her tongue is all about?"

He watched a door close somewhere inside her. "Grady . . ."

"What. 'Grady,' what."

"Just . . . don't, okay?"

"No, I want to hear it. 'Grady,' what. 'Grady, I fucked up'? 'Grady, our daughter is a walking car wreck and it's because I spent so much time drunk I didn't even care'?"

She wouldn't look at him. She smoked her cigarette and focused her gaze beyond him: on the lake, or on the mountains, or on some distant place he couldn't see.

"How about, 'Grady, I spent so much time banging Mitch while you were in jail that I forgot how to be a wife and a mother'?"

She shook her head; it was barely perceptible. "You're so goddamned mean," she said. "I was kinda hoping you'd of changed."

He leaned in close and spoke right into her ear. "No, fuck that. I'm more me than ever."


Grady showered—discovering that the substance on his hands was apparently impervious to soap—and the girls retreated to their rooms, nurturing their hurts, stranding him in the living room. He drank more coffee and flipped through the channels on TV. It was not unlike how he spent rec hour in jail, and he felt a profound self-pity at the realization. Goddamn evil bitches, he thought. I'm back a few days and they're already giving me the cold shoulder. It's disrespectful. He knew how to handle disrespect in prison; out here he felt emasculated by it.

He knew he should use this time to go out to the monster and start breaking it down. He'd only regret it if he allowed it to stay longer. But it would be gruesome, grueling work, and the very thought of it made his body sag into the couch. And anyway, it wasn't fair. These two weeks at the cabin were supposed to be for him, a celebration. He shouldn't have to climb up to his waist in fucking monster gore.

So instead he watched TV. He turned on VH1 and was pleased to see that the countdown of the 100 best Eighties songs he'd started watching in prison was still going on. It chewed through his day. From time to time Tina emerged from their bedroom and drifted silently past him into the kitchen, still wearing her robe; he heard the tinkle of ice in her glass and the hum of the freezer when she retrieved her vodka from it. Whenever she came back through he refused to look at her, and he supposed she returned the favor—certainly she said nothing to him. That was fine, though; he'd already proven he could live with hostile motherfuckers. She brought nothing new to the table.

Left to itself, though, his self-righteousness dissipated, and he fell into examining his own behavior. These women had been his beacons while he was in prison, and within days of his return he had driven them into hiding. He remembered it being like this sometimes, but it seemed worse now.

What's the matter with me? he thought. Why do I always fuck it up?

Eventually Sarah came out of her room. She was dressed to go outside, and she held a large pad of paper under her arm. She strode through the living room with a purpose and without a word. Just like her mother, Grady thought.

"Where are you going?"

She stopped, almost at the door, her back to him. She raised her face to the ceiling, as though imploring God. "Outside," she said.

"I can see that. Where to?"

She half turned, looking at him finally. "What does it matter?"

His teeth clenched. He stood up quickly, in a fluid motion: it was an abrupt and aggressive action, meant to convey threat, a holdover from the vocabulary of violence he'd spent years cultivating. "Because I'm your father," he said. "Don't you forget that."

She took a startled step backward; Grady felt a flare of satisfaction, and was immediately appalled at himself. He sat back down, scowling.

"I want to draw the monster," Sarah said, her voice markedly subdued.

"You—why would you want to do that?" All the anger had drained from him. He tried speaking to her now in a reasonable voice, the kind he thought a regular father might use.

She shrugged. She looked at the floor in front of her, looking for all the world like a punished child.

"Sarah, look at me."

Nothing.

He put some steel into it, not wanting her to make him angry again. "I said look at me."

She looked at him.

"You don't need to be going out there," he said.

She nodded. She tried to say something, failed, and tried again. "Okay."

But as she turned and headed back to her room, her face a cramped scrawl of defeat, his resolve washed away completely. He hadn't expected her to acquiesce so quickly, and he experienced a sudden need to show her that he could be giving, and kind. "You know what? Go ahead."

Sarah stopped again. "What?"

"Just go on. Go ahead."

She seemed to consider it for a moment, then said, "Okay," and turned back to the door. She walked out, shutting it quietly behind her.

She's so weak, he thought. How did this happen?

Despite the fact that she'd only been staying there three days, Sarah's room was a wreck. Her suitcase was open and clothes were stacked precariously on the bed, the ones she'd already worn strewn across the floor. He went into the little bathroom and looked in the medicine cabinet, which was empty, and into the trash can, where he found spent cigarettes. They were only half-consumed, which he supposed was a small blessing. He figured she was training herself to like them. Maybe there was still time to put a stop to it. He spent a futile moment at the sink, trying once more to clean his hands.

Back in the bedroom he opened the bureau drawers, thinking that he might find her diary. He was encouraged when he saw a spiral-bound notebook in one of them, until he opened it to find lists of chores and a draft of a letter to someone named Tamara about an impending trip—his mother-in-law's notebook, which made it eight years old at least. He looked under her mattress; he looked beneath her clothes in the suitcase. In a large zippered pouch on the lid of the suitcase he found large sheets of paper covered in pencil sketches.

They were drawings of a nude teenage boy. Her boyfriend, he guessed. The infamous Travis. He sat carefully on her bed and looked at them, breathing carefully, concentrating on holding his hands steady. He tried to reason with himself: the drawings were not lewd: he supposed they were classical poses. He even recognized, dimly, that the drawings were good. There was talent at work here. But mostly he felt a rising heat, a bloody flush of anger. A bead of sweat fell from his forehead and splashed onto the sketch, obliterating the boy's shoulder like a gunshot.

Well. No hiding it now.

He tore the drawings down the middle, turned them sideways and tore them again. He returned the quartered papers to the pouch in the suitcase, and determined that she would never, ever see that predatory little fuck again. He would see to it.

He left her room and stationed himself in front of the TV again. He couldn't decide what he should do. He would wait for her and reason with her. He would scream at her and put the fear of God into her. He would go into the other bedroom and beat Tina until she bled from her ears. He would let it all go, and not say a word. He would go outside and get the goddamned axe or chainsaw or whatever he could find and go down to the lake and lay into the moldering pile of garbage until his arms hurt too much to move, until he filled the air with blood, filled his lungs and his heart and his mouth with blood.

What he did was watch more TV. After a while he even began to pay attention to it. He forced himself to focus on whatever nonsense was on display, forced himself to listen to the commercials and consider the shiny plastic options they presented to him. It was a trick he'd cultivated in prison, a sort of meditation, to prevent himself from acting rashly, to keep himself out of trouble with the guards. Most of the time it worked.

He would not go down to the lake. He would not go into Tina's room, where she was steering herself into oblivion. He would sit down and be calm. It was easy.

He went into the kitchen and grabbed a bottle of vodka from the pantry. He left the one in the freezer for Tina; unlike her, he liked to feel the burn.


A couple of hours passed. Sarah stayed gone. He killed half the bottle. The TV show became something else, then something else again, and his thoughts blundered about until they found Mitch. Tina had told him about Mitch while he was in jail. She started seeing him after he'd been in about four years, well after Sarah stopped coming to see him. He'd received the news stoically—he was proud of himself for that, even to this day. He inflicted catastrophic violence on some guy later that day, sure, but no one who wasn't going to get it anyway. On the whole he thought he handled it all exceptionally well. And good news: Mitch got dumped after about six months.

Grady told himself he could live with it, and he did.

But it ate at him. Just a little bit.

Now seemed as good a time as any to explore his feelings on this matter with his wife. To have an intimate discussion with her. It might serve to repair some of this breakage between them. Grady lifted himself off the couch and plotted a course to the bedroom. He placed his hand on the wall to steady himself; the floor was trying to buck him. He would show it. He took a few lurching steps and halted, one arm held aloft for balance. When it seemed that doom had been skirted, he took a few more steps and reached the far wall. There was a window there, and he cracked it for some fresh air. The sun was fail-ing, little pools of nighttime gathering beneath the trees. He smelled something faintly sweet riding the air, and he breathed deeply and gratefully before he realized it must be the moldering corpse of the monster. Shaken, he pulled away from the window and went into the bedroom.

Tina was awake, lying flat on the bed and staring at the ceiling. A photo album was open at her feet; some of the pictures had been removed and spread atop the covers. When he came in she rolled her head to look at him, and flopped an arm in his direction. "Hey babe," she said.

"Hey."

He sat heavily on the bed. The room was mostly dark, with only a faint yellow light leaking through the curtains. He picked up one of the loose photos: it was a picture of her father standing by the lake, holding up a big fish. "What the hell are you looking at?"

She plucked the picture from his hand and tossed it to the floor, laughing at him. "'What the hell are you looking at?'" she said, rolling her body onto his legs.

"Don't do that."

"'Don't do that.'"

He laughed despite himself, grabbing a handful of her hair and giving it a gentle tug.

"Ain't you mad no more?" she asked, her fingers working at the button of his pants.

"Shut up, bitch," he said, but affectionately, and she responded as though he'd just recited a line of verse, shedding her robe and lifting herself over and onto him, so that he felt as though he were sliding into a warm sea. He closed his eyes and exhaled, feeling it down to his fingertips.

They moved roughly, urgently, breathing in the musk of each other, breathing in too the smell of the pines and the lake and the dead monster, this last growing in power until it occluded the others, until it filled his sinuses, his head, his body, until it seemed nothing existed except that smell and the awful thing that made it, until it seemed he was its source, the wellspring of all the foulness of the earth, and when he spent himself into her he thought for a wretched moment that he had somehow injected it with the possibility of new life.

She rolled off of him, saying something he couldn't hear. Grady put his hand over his face, breathed through his nose. Tina rested her head on his chest, and he put his nose to her hair, filling it with something recognizable and good. They lay together for long moments, their limbs a motionless tangle, glowing like marble in the fading light.

"Why couldn't you wait for me?" he said quietly.

She tensed. For a while he could hear nothing but her breath, and the creaking of the trees outside as the wind moved through them. She rubbed her fingers through the hair on his chest.

"Please don't ask me that," she said.

He was quiet, waiting for her.

"I don't know why I did it. I don't know a whole lot about that time. But I just don't ever want to talk about it. I wish it never happened."

"Okay," he said. It wasn't good enough. But he was just drunk enough to realize that nothing would be. He would have to figure out whether or not he could live with it. It was impossible to say, just now. So he lay there with her and felt the weight of her body against his. When he closed his eyes he imagined himself beneath deep water, part of some ruined structure of broken gray stone, like some devastated row of teeth.

"I should make dinner," Tina said. "Sarah's probably hungry."

Her name went off inside him like a depth charge. He lurched upright, ignoring the swimming sensation in his brain. "Sarah," he said. "She went out."

"What?"

"To that thing. She went out to that thing."

Tina seemed confused. "When?"

"Hours ago." He swung his legs out of bed. "God damn it. I've been drunk!"

"Grady, calm down. I'm sure she's fine."

He hurried through the living room, his heart crashing through his chest, a fear he had not believed possible crowing raucously in his head. He pushed her door open.

She was there, illuminated by a slice of light from the living room, lying on her belly, her feet by the headboard. Her arms were tucked under her body for warmth. Her suitcase was open, and the pictures he had destroyed were on the floor beside it.

"Sarah?" he whispered, and stepped inside. He placed his hand on her back, felt the heat unfurling from her body, felt the rise and fall of her breath. He crept around the bed and looked at her face. Her eyes were closed and gummed by tears; her mouth was slightly parted. A little damp pool of saliva darkened the blanket underneath. The rings in her ears caught the light from the living room.

He stroked her hair, moving it off of her forehead and hooking it behind her ear. Anything could have happened to her, he thought. While I was drinking myself stupid in the other room, anything could have happened to her.

Tina's voice came in from the other room. "Grady? Is she all right?"

Christ. I'm just like her. I'm just as fucking bad. He went to the door and poked his head out. "Yeah. She's sleeping."

Tina smiled at him and shook her head. "I told you," she said.

"Yeah." He went back into the room. He pulled off Sarah's shoes and socks, slid her jacket off her shoulders. After a lot of careful maneuvering he managed to get her turned around and underneath the covers without waking her. He leaned over to kiss her on the forehead, and smelled the vodka on his own breath. Self-loathing hit him like a wrecking ball. He scrambled into her bathroom and barely made it before puking into the toilet, clutching the bowl with both hands, one leg looking weakly for purchase behind him. He'd had nothing but vodka and coffee all day, so there wasn't much to throw up.

When he felt able, he flushed the toilet and headed back to the bedroom. He leaned over and picked up the torn pictures, so he could throw them away. Beneath them he found the new ones, the ones she'd spent all day working on.

He didn't recognize them at first. She'd used colored pencils, and he initially thought he was looking at a house made of rainbows. Upon closer inspection, though, he realized that she'd drawn the dead monster: as a kaleidoscope, as a grounded sun. His mind reeled. He dropped it to the ground and here was the monster again, rendered larger than it was in real life, its mouth the gaping Gothic arches of a cathedral, its eyes stained glass, ignited by sunlight. There was another, and another, each depicting it as something beautiful, warm, and bright.

Why couldn't she get it? Why was she forever romanticizing vileness? His breath was getting short. He rubbed his temples, his body physically rocking as waves of anger rolled through him. She was just stupid, apparently. It was too late. Maybe he'd fucked her up, maybe Tina did, but the damage was done. She'd have to be protected her whole goddamned life.

Might as well start now, he thought. Tina was in the living room as he walked through it, shrugging into his jacket.

"Where are you going?"

"Is the shed locked?"

"What?"

"*Is the shed fucking locked?*"

"I, no, I—"

"Good. Stay here."

When he opened the front door the cold slammed into him like a truck. The temperature had dropped precipitously with the sun. He paused to catch his breath, then jumped down the stairs and headed around back to the shed. He slid the door open and flipped on the light. Inside was a dark, cobwebby tomb of stacked wood and garden appliances with the untroubled appearance of dead Egyptian kings. No chainsaw was evident, but he did find an axe leaning against the wall behind a rusting lawnmower. He reached gingerly through a shroud of webs, wary of spiders, and grasped the handle. He pulled it out, trailing dust and ghostly banners.

It had changed since this morning. It actually was shedding light, for one thing, though it was a dim phosphorescence, the result of some strange fungus or bacterium running amuck through its innards. The creature looked like some ghastly oversized nightlight. The gash that was either a mouth or a wound had borne fruit: a weird and vibrant flora spilled from it like fruit from a cornucopia, pale protuberances with growths like outstretched arms listing this way and that, a dozen vegetable christs. Life abounded here: small chitinous animals hurried busily to and fro, conducting their miserable business in tunnels and passageways in the body, provided for them by nature or their own savage industry; a cloud of insects, drunk on the very perfume which had driven him into fits, alternately settling on its carcass and lifting away again in graceful curtains, like wind blowing through a wheatfield.

Grady raised his axe and took a few tentative steps toward it.

Something moved near him: a raccoon startled from its feast and gone crashing into the underbrush. The flesh around where it had been eating sloughed away, and more light spilled into the forest: hundreds of small insects, their backs coated with the glowing fluids of this dead thing, moved about the wound like boiling suns.

The axe was heavy, so he let it drop. He couldn't process what he was seeing. He had to figure it out. He sat down in the mud several feet away from all that incandescent motion and stared at it for a while.

He looked at the palms of his hands. They cast light.

# The Way Station

*Beltrane awakens to the smell of baking bread.* It smells like that huge bakery on MLK that he liked to walk past on mornings before the sun came up, when daylight was just a paleness behind buildings, and the smell of fresh bread leaked from the grim industrial slab like the promise of absolute love.

He stirs in his cot. The cot and the smell disorient him; his body is accustomed to the worn cab seat, with its tears in the upholstery and its permanent odor of contained humanity, as though the car, over the many years of carrying people about, had finally leached some fundamental ingredient from them. But the coarse, grainy blanket reminds him that he is in St. Petersburg, Florida, now. Far from home. Looking for Lila. Someone sitting on a nearby cot, back turned to him, is speaking urgently under his breath, rocking on the thin mattress and making it sing. Around them more cots are lined in rank and file, with scores of people sleeping or trying to sleep.

There are no windows, but the night is a presence in here, filling even the bright places.

"You smell that, man?" he says, sitting up.

His neighbor goes still and silent, and turns to face him. He's younger than Beltrane, with a huge salt-and-pepper beard and grime deeply engrained into the lines of his face. "What?"

"Bread."

The guy shakes his head and gives him his back again. "Maaa-aaaan," he says. "*Sick* of these crazy motherfuckers."

"Did they pass some out? I'm just sayin, man. I'm hungry, you know?"

"We all hungry, bitch! Whyn't you take your ass to sleep!"

Beltrane falls back onto the bed, defeated. After a moment the other man resumes his barely audible incantations, his obsessive rocking. Meanwhile the smell has grown even stronger, overpowering the musk of sweat and urine that saturates the homeless shelter. Sighing, he folds his hands over his chest, and discovers that the blanket is wet and cold.

"What . . . ?"

He pulls it down to find a large, damp patch on his shirt. He hikes the shirt up to his shoulders and discovers a large square hole in the center of his chest. The smell of bread blows from it like a wind. The edges are sharp and clean, not like a wound at all. Tentatively, he probes it with his fingers: they come away damp, and when he brings them to his nose they have the ripe, deliquescent odor of river water. He places his hand over the opening and feels water splash against his palm. Poking inside, he encounters sharp metal angles and slippery stone.

Beltrane lurches from his bed and stumbles quickly for the door to the bathroom, leaving a wake of jarred cots and angry protest. He pushes through the door and heads straight for the mirrors over a row of dirty sinks. He lifts his shirt.

The hole in his chest reaches right through him. Gas lamps shine blearily through rain. Deep water runs down the street and spills out onto his skin. New Orleans has put a finger through his heart.

"Oh, no," he says softly, and raises his eyes to his own face. His face is a wide street, garbage-blown, with a dead streetlight and rats scrabbling along the walls. A spray of rain mists the air in front of him, pebbling the mirror.

He knows this street. He's walked it many times in his life, and as he leans closer to the mirror he finds that he is walking it now, home again in his old city, the bathroom and the strange shelter behind him and gone. He takes a right into an alley. Somewhere to his left is a walled cemetery, with its above-ground tombs giving it the look of a city for the dead; and next to it will be the projects, where some folks string Christmas lights along their balconies even in the summertime. He follows his accustomed path and turns right onto Claiborne Avenue. And there's his old buddy Craig, waiting for him still.


Craig was leaning against the plate-glass window of his convenience store, two hours closed, clutching a greasy brown paper bag in his left hand, with his gray head hanging and a cigarette stuck to his lips. A few butts were scattered by his feet. The neighborhood was asleep under the arch of the I-10 overpass: a row of darkened shop-fronts receded down Claiborne Avenue, the line broken by the colorful lights of the Good Friends Bar spilling onto the sidewalk. The highway above them was mostly quiet now, save the occasional hiss of late-night travelers hurtling through the darkness toward mysterious ends. Beltrane, sixty-four and homeless, moseyed up to him. He stared at Craig's shirt pocket, trying to see if the cigarette pack was full enough to risk asking for one.

Craig watched him as he approached. "I almost went home," he said curtly.

"You wouldn't leave old 'Trane!"

"The hell I wouldn't. See if I'm here next time."

Beltrane sidled up next to him, putting his hands in the pockets of his thin coat, which he always wore, in defiance of the Louisiana heat. "I got held up," he said.

"You what? You got held up? What do you got to do that you got held up?"

Beltrane shrugged. He could smell the contents of the bag Craig held, and his stomach started to move around inside him a little.

"What, you got a date? Some little lady gonna take you out tonight?"

"Come on, man. Don't make fun of me."

"Then don't be late!" Craig pressed the bag against his chest. Beltrane took it, keeping his gaze on the ground. "I do this as a favor. You make me wait outside my own goddamn shop I just won't do it no more. You gonna get my ass *shot.*"

Beltrane stood there and tried to look ashamed. But the truth was, he wasn't much later than usual. Craig came down on him like this every couple of months or so, and if he was going to keep getting food from him he was just going to have to take it. A couple years ago Beltrane had worked for him, pushing the broom around the store and shucking oysters when they were in season, and for some reason Craig had taken a liking to him. Maybe it was the veteran thing; maybe it was something more personal. When Beltrane started having his troubles again, Craig finally had to fire him, but made some efforts to see that he didn't starve. Beltrane didn't know why the man cared, but he wasn't moved to examine the question too closely. He figured Craig had his reasons and they were his own. Sometimes those reasons caused him to speak harshly. That was all right.

He opened the bag and dug out some fried shrimp. They'd gone cold and soggy, but the smell of them just about buckled his knees, and he closed his eyes as he chewed his first mouthful.

"Where you been sleepin at night, 'Trane? My boy Ray tells me he ain't seen you down by Decatur in a while."

Beltrane gestured uptown, in the opposite direction of Decatur Street and the French Quarter. "They gave me a broke-down cab."

"Who? Them boys at United? That's better than the Quarter?"

Beltrane nodded. "They's just a bunch a damn fucked-up white kids in the Quarter. Got all kinds a metal shit in their face. They smell bad, man."

Craig shook his head, leaning against the store window and lighting himself another cigarette. "Oh, they smell bad, huh. I guess I heard it all now."

Beltrane gestured at the cigarette. "Can I have one?"

"*Hell* no. So you sleeping in some junk heap now. You gone down a long way since you worked for me here, you know that? You got to pull your shit together, man."

"I know, I know."

"Listen to me, 'Trane. Are you listening to me?"

"I know what you gonna say."

"Well listen to me anyway. I know you're fucked in the head. I got that. I know you don't remember shit half the time, and you got your imaginary friends you like to talk to. But you got to get a handle on things, man."

Beltrane nodded, half smiling. This speech again. "Yeah, I know."

"No you *don't* know. 'Cause if you *did*, you would go down to the VA hospital and get yourself some damn pills for whatever's wrong with you and get off the goddamn street. You will fucking *die* out here, 'Trane, you keep fucking around like this."

Beltrane nodded again, and turned to leave. "You better get on home, Craig. Might get shot out here."

"*Now* who's making fun," Craig said. He tried to push himself off his window, but the glass had grown into his head. His shoulders were stuck, too. "It's too late," he said. "I can't go home. I'm stuck here forever now. God damn it!"

"I'm goin up to the white neighborhood," Beltrane said. He avoided looking at Craig, turned his back to him and started to walk uptown.

"Yeah, you go on and get drunk! See what that'll fix!"

"I'm goin to find that little Ivy, man. She always hang out up there. This time I'm gonna get that girl."

"I can't understand you anymore. My ears are gone." And it was true: Craig had been almost wholly absorbed by his window now, or maybe he had merged with it. In any case, his body was mostly gone. Only the contours of his face and his small rounded shoulders stood out from the glass; his lower legs and feet still stuck out near the ground. But he was mostly just an image in the glass now.

Beltrane hurried down the street, feeling the beginnings of a cool wind start to kick up. He glanced behind him once, looking for Craig's shape, but he didn't see anything.

Just the empty storefront staring back at him.


Beltrane stands in front of the mirror and watches his face for movement. He exerts great concentration to hold himself still: the slopes and angles of his face, the wiry gray coils of beard growing up over his cheeks, the wide round nostrils—even his eyelids—are as unmoving as hard earth. The skin beneath his eyes is heavy and layered, and the fissures in his face are deep—but nothing seems out of place. Nothing is doing anything it isn't supposed to be doing.

He's standing over one of the sinks in the shelter's bathroom. It has five partitioned stalls, most of which have lost their doors, and a bank of dingy gray urinals on the opposite wall. After a moment the door opens and one of the volunteers pokes his head in. When he sees Beltrane in there alone, he comes in all the way and lets the door swing closed behind him. He's a heavy man with high yellow skin, a few dark skin tags standing out on his neck like tiny beetles. Beltrane has seen him around a little bit, over the couple of days he's been here, kneeling down sometimes to pray with folks that were willing.

"You all right?" the volunteer asks.

Beltrane just looks at him. He can't think of anything to say, so after a moment he just turns his gaze back to the mirror.

"The way you charged in here, I thought you might be in trouble." The volunteer stays in his place by the door.

Beltrane looks back at him. "You see anything wrong with my face?"

The man squints, but comes no closer. "No. Looks okay to me." When Beltrane doesn't add anything else, he says, "You know, we have strict policies on drug use in here."

"I ain't on drugs. I got this thing here . . . I don't know, I don't know." He lifts his shirt and turns to the volunteer, who displays no reaction. "Can you see this?" he asks.

"That street there? Yes, I can see it."

Beltrane says, "I think I'm haunted."

The man says nothing for a moment. Then, "Is that New Orleans?"

Beltrane nods.

"I guess you're here from Katrina?"

"Yeah, that's right. It fucked my world up, man. Everybody gone."

The man nods. "Most people from New Orleans are going up to Baton Rouge, or to Houston. What brings you all the way out here?"

"My girl. My girl lives here. I'm gonna move in with her."

"Your girlfriend?"

"No, my *girl!* My daughter!"

"You've been here two days already, haven't you? Where is she?"

"She don't know I'm coming. I got to find her." Beltrane stares at himself. His face is dry. His hair is dry. He lifts his shirt to stare at the hole there one more time, but it's gone now; he runs his hand over the old brown flesh, the curly gray hairs.

The volunteer says nothing for a moment. Then, "How long has it been since you've seen her?"

Beltrane looks down into the sink. The porcelain around the drain is chipped and rusty. A distant gurgling sound rises from the pipes, as though something is alive down there, in the bowels of the city. He has to think for a minute. "Twenty-three years," he says finally.

The volunteer's face is still. "That's a long time."

"She got married."

"Is that when she moved here?"

"I got to find her. I got to find my little girl."

The volunteer seems to consider this; then he opens the door to the common area. "My name's Ron Davis. I'm the pastor at the Trinity Baptist, just down the street a few blocks. If you're all done in here, why don't you come down there with me. I think I might be able to help you."

Beltrane looks at him. "A pastor? Come on, man. I don't want to hear about God tonight."

"That's fine. We don't have to talk about God."

"If I leave they won't let me back in. They just give up my cot to someone else."

Davis shakes his head. "You won't have to come back tonight. You can sleep at the church. If we're lucky, you won't ever have to come back here. If we're not, I'll make sure you have a bed tomorrow night." He smiles. "It'll be okay. I do have some influence here, you know."

They leave the shelter together, stepping into the close heat of the Florida night. The air out here smells strongly of the sea, so much that Beltrane experiences a brief thrill in his heart, a sense of being in a place both strange and new. To their left, several blocks down Central Avenue, he can see the tall masts of sail boats in the harbor gathered like a copse of birch trees, pale and ethereal in the darkness. To their right the city extends in a plain of concrete and light, softly glowing overpasses arcing over the street in grace notes of steel. People hunch along the sidewalks, they sleep in the small alcoves of shop doors. Some of them lift their heads as the two men emerge. One of them tugs at Beltrane's pant leg as he walks by. "Hey. Are you leaving? Is they a bed in there?"

Davis says something to the man, but Beltrane ignores them both. He hopes the walk to the church is not long. The pleasant sense of disorientation he felt just a moment ago is giving way to anxiety. The buildings seem too impersonal; the faces are all strange.

He looks up at the sky—and there, in the thunderheads, he finds something familiar.


Piling rainclouds and the cool winds which precede a storm made the walk uptown more pleasant. Rain was not a deterrent, especially in the summer months when the storms in New Orleans were sudden, violent, and quickly over. Low gray clouds obscured the night sky, their great bellies illuminated from time to time by huge, silent explosions of lightning. Beltrane's bones hummed in this weather, as though with a live current. He made his way out of the darkened neighborhood of the Tremé and into the jeweled glow of New Orleans' Central Business District, where lights glittered even when the buildings were empty. The streetcar chimed from some unseen distance, roaring along the unobstructed tracks like a charging animal. He walked along them, past the banks and the hotels until at last he hit the wide boulevard of St. Charles Avenue and entered the Lower Garden District. The neutral ground—the grassy swath dividing the avenue into uptown and downtown traffic—was wide enough here to accommodate two streetcar tracks running side by side. Palm trees had been planted here long ago by some starry-eyed city planner. A half mile ahead they gave way to the huge, indigenous oaks, which had seen the palm trees planted and would eventually watch them die. They stood like ancient gods, protecting New Orleans from the wild skies above her.


"Here we are," Ron says, and Beltrane drifts to a stop beside him. There are no trees here. There are no streetcars.

The Trinity Baptist Church is just one door in a strip mall, sandwiched between a Christian bookstore and a temp agency. The glass of its single window is smudged and dirty; deep red curtains are closed on the inside, and the corpses of moths and flies are piled on the windowsill. Ron takes a moment to unlock the door. Then he reaches inside and flips on the light.

"My office is in the back," he says. "Come on in."

They walk through a large, open area, with rows of folding chairs arranged neatly before a lectern. The linoleum floor is dirty and scuffed with years' worth of rubber soles. Ron opens a plywood door in the rear of the room and ushers Beltrane into his cramped office. He seats himself behind a desk which takes up most of the space in here and directs Beltrane to sit down in one of the two chairs on the other side. Then he switches on a computer.

While it boots up, he says, "We'll look online and see if we can find her. What's your name?"

"Henry Beltrane."

"You said she was married. Will she still have your name?"

"Um . . . Delacroix. That's her husband's name."

Davis's fingers tap the keys, and he hunches closer to the screen. He pauses, and begins to type some more. "Twenty-three years is a long time," he says. "How old would she be about now? Forty?"

"Forty-five," Beltrane says. "Forty-five years old." It's the first time he's said it aloud. It works like a spell, calling up the gulf of years between now and the time he last saw her, when he was drunk in a bar and she was trying one more time to save his life.

*Dad?* she'd said. *We're leaving. Four more days. We're doing it.*

He'd turned his back to her then. There'd been a television behind the bar, and he fixed his eyes to it. *Have a good trip,* he said.

*It's not a trip. Do you understand? We're moving there. I'm moving away, Dad.*
*Yeah, I know.*

She grabbed his shoulders and turned him on his stool so that he had to look at her. *Daddy, please.*

He watched her for a moment, shaping her face out of the unraveling world. He was so drunk. The sun was still up, filtering through the dusty windows of the bar. Her eyes were tearing up. *What,* he said. *What. What you want from me?*

Davis releases a long sigh, and leans back in his chair. "I got a Sam and Lila Delacroix. That sound right?"

Beltrane's heart turns over. "That's her. Lila. That's her."

Davis jots the address and phone number down on a sticky note, and passes it across to Beltrane. "Guess it's your lucky night," he says, though his voice is flat.

Beltrane stares at the number in his hand, a faint, disbelieving smile on his lips. "You call her for me?"

Davis leans back in his chair and smiles. "What, right now? It's almost midnight, Mr. Beltrane. You can't call her now. She'll be in bed."

Beltrane nods, absorbing this.

"Look, I keep a mattress in the closet for when I don't make it home. I can pull it out for you. You can crash right here tonight."

Beltrane nods again. The thought of a mattress overwhelms him, and he feels his eyes tearing up. His mind skips ahead to tomorrow, to wondering about how soft the beds might be in Lila's home, if she'll let him stay. He wonders what it will feel like to wake up in the morning and smell coffee and breakfast. To have someone say kind things to him, and be happy to see him. He knew all those things once. They were a long time ago.

"You have a problem," Davis says.

The words push through the dream, and it's gone. He waits for his throat to open up again, so he can speak. He says, "I think I'm haunted."

Davis keeps his eyes locked on him. "I think so too," he says.

Beltrane can't think of what else to say. His hand rubs absentmindedly over his chest. He knows he can't see his daughter while this is happening to him.

"I was haunted once, too," Davis says quietly. He opens a drawer in his desk and withdraws a pack of cigarettes. He extends one to Beltrane and keeps one for himself. "Then the ghost went away."

Beltrane stares at him with an awed hope as Davis slowly fishes through his pockets for a lighter. "How you get rid of it?"

Davis lights both cigarettes. Beltrane wants to grab the man, but instead he takes a draw, and the nicotine hits his bloodstream. A spike of euphoria rolls through him with a magnificent energy.

"I don't want to tell you that," Davis says. "I want to tell you why you should keep it. And why you shouldn't go see your daughter tomorrow."

Beltrane's mouth opens. He's half smiling. "You crazy," he says softly.

"What do you think of, when you think of New Orleans?"

He feels a cramp in his stomach. His joints begin sending telegraphs of distress. He can't let this happen. "Fuck you. I'm leaving." Davis is still as Beltrane hoists himself out of his chair. "The shelter won't let you back in. You said it yourself, you gave up the bed when you left. Where are you going to go?"

"I'll go to Lila's. It don't matter if it's late. She'll take me in."

"Will she? With streets winding through your body? With lamps in your eyes? With rain blowing out of your heart? No. She will slam that door in your face and lock it tight. She will think she is visited by something from hell. She will not take you in."

Beltrane stands immobile, one hand still clutching the chair, his eyes fixed not on anything in this room but instead on that awful scene. He hasn't seen Lila's face in twenty years, but he can see it now, contorted in fear and disgust at the sight of him. He feels something shift in his body, something harden in his limbs. He squeezes his eyes shut and wills his body to keep its shape.

"Please," says Davis. "Sit back down."

Beltrane sits.

"You're in between places right now. People think it's the ghost that lives between places, but it's not. It's us. Tell me what you think of when you think of New Orleans."

Moving up St. Charles Avenue, Beltrane arrived at the Avenue Pub, which shed light onto the sidewalk through its open French doors and cast music and voices into the night. He peered through the windows before entering, to see who was working. The good ones would let him come in, have a few drinks. The others would turn him away at the door, forcing him to decide between walking all the way back down to the French Quarter for his booze, or just calling it a night and going back to his wrecked car at the cab station.

He was in luck; it was John.

He stepped inside and was greeted by people calling his name. He held up a hand in greeting, getting into character. This was a white bar. There were certain expectations he'd have to fulfill if he was going to get his drinks. Some college kid—he had short hair and always smelled of perfume; he could never remember his name—grabbed his hand in a powerful squeeze. "'Trane! My *dog!* What up, dude?"

"Awright, awright," Beltrane said, letting the kid crush his hand. It was going to hurt all night.

The kid yelled over the crowd. "Yo John, set me up one of them shots for 'Trane here!"

John smiled. "You're evil, dude."

"Oh, whatever, man! Pour me one too! I can't let him go down that road all by hisself!"

Beltrane maneuvered to an open spot at the bar beside a pretty white girl he'd never seen before and an older guy wearing an electrician's jumpsuit. The girl made a disgusted noise and inched away from him. The electrician nodded at him and said his name. The college kid joined him in a moment with two milky gray shots in his hand. He pushed the larger one at Beltrane.

"Dude! I'm worried, bro. I don't know if you're man enough for a shot like this."

"Shiiiit. I a man!"

"This is a man's drink, dog!"

"Dat's what I am! I a man!"

"Then do the shot!"

He did the shot. It tasted vile, of course: like paint thinner and yogurt. They always gave him some horrible shit to drink. But it was real booze, and it slammed into his brain like a wrecking ball. He coughed and wiped his mouth with the back of his hand.

The college kid slapped his back. "Shit, 'Trane! You okay? I thought you said you was a man!"

He tried to talk, but he couldn't get his throat to unclench. He ended up just waving his hand dismissively.

Beltrane screwed a bleary eye in the bartender's direction, who moved in a series of ripples and left a ghostly trail in his wake. A beer seemed to sprout from the bartop like a weed. He held out the bag of shrimp he'd gotten earlier. "Heat this up for me, John."

When John came back a few minutes later with the bag, Beltrane said, "You seen Ivy tonight?"

"She was here earlier. You still trying to hit that, you pervert?"

Beltrane just laughed. He clutched his beer and settled into his customary reverie as bar life broke and flowed around him, wrapping him in warmth, like a slow-moving river. He downed the shots as they appeared before him and concentrated on keeping them down. Somewhere in the drift of the night a girl materialized beside him, her back half turned to him as she spoke with somebody on her other side. She had a tattoo of a Japanese print on her shoulder, which dipped below the line of her sleeveless white shirt. She was delicate and beautiful. He brushed her arm with the back of his hand, trying to make it seem accidental, and she turned to face him.

"Hey, 'Trane," she said. Her eyes shed a warm yellow light. He wanted to touch her, but there was a divide he couldn't cross.

"We all God's children," he said.

"Yeah, I know." She looked at the boy she was talking to and rolled her eyes. When she looked at him again she had raised windows for eyes, with curtains blowing out of them, framing a yellow-lit room. Below them, her face declined in wet shingles, flowing with little rivulets of rainwater. It took him a moment to realize the water was flowing from inside her. Behind her, her friend rose to his feet; wood and plaster cracked and split as he stood. His eyes were windows, too, but the lights there had been blown out. Water gushed from them. The bar had gone silent; in his peripheral vision he saw that he was ringed with wet, shining faces.

A figure moved to the window in the girl's face. It was backlit; he couldn't make out who it was. Water was rising around his feet, soaking through his shoes, making him cold.

Davis says, "There's some people I want you to meet." His voice is so soft Beltrane can barely hear it. Davis is sitting on the edge of his desk, looming over him. His eyes are moist.

Beltrane blinks. "I got to get out of here."

"Just wait. Please?"

"You can't keep me here. I ain't a prisoner."

"No, I know. Your . . . your ghost is very strong. I've never seen one that was a—a city, before."

Beltrane is suddenly uncomfortable with Davis's proximity to him. "What you doing this close? Back off a me, man."

Davis takes a deep breath and slides off his desk, moving back to his side of it. He collapses into his chair. "There's some people I want you to meet," he says. "Will you stay just a little bit longer?"

The thought of going outside into this strange city does not appeal to Beltrane. He doesn't know the neighborhood, doesn't know which places are safe for homeless people to go and which places are off-limits—whether due to police, or thugs, or just because it's someone else's turf. He was always safe in New Orleans, which he knew as well as he knew his own face. But new places are dangerous.

"You got another cigarette?" he says. Davis seems to relax a little, and passes one to him. After it's lit, he says, "How come I can't get rid of it?"

"You can," says Davis. "It's just that you shouldn't. Do you—do you really know what a ghost is, Mr. Beltrane?"

"This must be where you start preaching."

"A ghost is something that fills a hole inside you, where you lost something. It's a memory. Sometimes it can be painful, and sometimes it can be scary. Sometimes it's hard to tell where the ghost ends and real life begins. I know you know what I mean."

Beltrane just looks away, affecting boredom. But he can feel his heart turning in his chest, and sweat bristling along his scalp.

"But if you get rid of it, Mr. Beltrane, if you *get rid of it*, you have *nothing* left." He pauses. "You just have a hole."

Beltrane darts a glance at him. Davis is leaning over his desk, urgency scrawled across his face. He's sweating, too, and his eyes look sunken, as though someone has jerked them back into his head from behind. His appearance unnerves Beltrane, and he turns away.

"Emptiness. Silence. Is that really better? You need to think carefully about what you decide you can live without, Mr. Beltrane." He pauses for a moment. When Beltrane stays silent, he leans even closer and asks, "What do you really think is going to happen when you make that call tomorrow?"

A cold pulse of fear flows through Beltrane's body. But before he can think of a response, a sound reaches them through the closed door. People are entering the church from the street.

Davis smiles suddenly. It's an artificial smile, manic, out of all proportion to any possible stimulus. "They're here! Come on!"

He leads him into the large room with the lectern and the rows of chairs. Two people—a young, slender Latina woman and an older, obese white man—have just entered and are standing uncertainly by the door. Although they're dressed in simple, cheap clothing, it's immediately obvious that they're not homeless. They both stare at Beltrane as he approaches behind the pastor.

"Come on, everybody," Davis says, gesturing to the front row of chairs. "Let's sit down."

Davis arranges a chair to face them, and soon they are all sitting in a clumsy circle. "These are the people I wanted you to meet," he says. "This is Maria and Evan. They're haunted, too."

Maria tries to form a smile beneath eyes that are sunken and dark, like moon craters or like cigarette burns. She seems long out of practice. Evan is staring intently at the floor. He's breathing heavily through his nose with a reedy, pistoning regularity. His forehead is glistening with sweat.

"I'm trying to start a little group here, you know? People with your sort of problem."

"This is how we gonna get rid of it?" Beltrane asks.

Davis and Maria exchange glances.

"They don't want to get rid of them," Davis says. "That's why they're here." He turns to the others. "Mr. Beltrane came here from New Orleans. He's looking for his daughter."

Maria gives him a crushed look. "Oh, pobrecito," she says. The news seems to affect her deeply: her face clouds over, and her eyes well up. Beltrane looks away, embarrassed for her, and ashamed at his own optimism.

"His ghost is a city."

This seems to catch even Evan's attention, who looks at him for the first time. "I'm the Ghost of Christmas Past," Evan says, and barks a laugh. "My family died in a fire two days after Christmas. The fucking tree! It's like a joke, right?"

Davis pats Evan on the knee. "We'll get to it, my friend. We will. But first we have to help him understand."

"Right, right. But it wants to come out. It wants to come out right now."

"Mr. Beltrane thinks he lost his city in the flood," Davis continues.

"I did lose it!" Beltrane shouts, feeling both scared and angry to be among these people. "After Katrina came, I lost everything! Craig moved away after his place flooded! Places I go to are all shut down. The people all gone. Ivy . . . Ivy, she . . . she was in this empty old house she used to crash in. . . ." His throat closes, and he stops there.

Davis waits a moment, then puts his hand on his shoulder. "But it's not really gone, though, is it?" He touches Beltrane on the forehead, and then on his chest. "Is it?"

Beltrane shakes his head.

"And if it ever does go away, well, God help you then. Because you will be all by yourself. You will be all alone." He pauses. "You don't want that. Nobody wants that."

Evan makes a noise and puts a hand over his mouth.

"I had enough of this crazy shit," Beltrane says, and stands. Davis opens his mouth, but before he can speak the room is filled with the scent of cloves and cinnamon. The effect is so jarring that Beltrane nearly loses his balance.

Evan doubles over in his seat, hands over his face, his big body shuddering with sobs. The smell pours from him. Smoke leaks from between his fingers, spreading in cobwebby wreaths over his head. Beltrane wants to run, but he's never seen this kind of thing in anyone but himself before, and he's transfixed.

"Oh, here it comes," Davis says, not to the others but to himself, his eyes glassy and fixed, staring at Evan. "That's all right, just let it out. You have to let it come out. You have to hold on to what's left. Never let it go." He looks at Maria. "Can you feel him, Maria? Can you?"

Maria nods. Her eyes are filled with tears. Her hands are clutching her stomach, and Beltrane watches as it grows beneath them, accompanied by a powerful, sickly odor that he does not recognize right away. When he does he feels a buckling inside, the turning over of some essential organ or element, and he is overwhelmed by a powerful need to flee.

"Will you get rid of this?" Davis is saying, his face so close to Maria's they might be lovers. "Will you get rid of your child, Maria? Who could ask that of you? Who would dare?"

Beltrane backs up a step and falls over a chair, sprawling to the floor in a clatter of noise and his own flailing arms. There's a sudden, spiking pain as his elbow takes the brunt of his weight. The air grows steadily colder; the appalling mix of cinnamon and desiccated flesh roots into his nose. Davis kneels between the others, one hand touching each body, and once again his features seem to be tugging inward, even his round stomach is drawing in, as though something empty, some starving need, is glutting itself on this weird energy; as though there's a black hole inside him, filling its belly with light.

"Please God, just let it come," Davis says.

Beltrane tries to scramble to his feet and slips. A large, growing puddle of Mississippi River water surrounds him. It soaks his clothes. He tries again, making it to his feet this time, and staggers to the door. He pushes his way outside, into the warm, humid night, and without waiting to see if they're following he lurches further down the street, away from the church, away from the shelter, until an alleyway opens like a throat and he turns gratefully into it. He manages to make it a few more feet before he collapses to his knees. He doesn't know anymore if the pain he feels is coming from arthritis or from the ghost which has wrapped itself like a vine around his bones.

Across the alley, in the alcove of a delivery door, he sees a mound of clothing and a duffel bag: this is somebody's roost. A shadow falls over him as a figure stops in the mouth of the alley. The city light makes a dark shape of it, a negative space. "What you doin here?" it says.

Beltrane closes his eyes: an act of surrender. "I just restin, man," he says, almost pleads. "I ain't stayin."

"You don't belong here."

"Come on, man. Just let me rest a minute. I ain't gonna stay. Can't you see what's happening to me?"

When he opens his eyes, he is alone. He exhales, and it almost sounds like a sob. "I wanna go home," he whispers. "I wanna go home." He runs his hands through his hair, dislodging drowned corpses, which tumble into his lap.

Beltrane left the Avenue Pub behind, well and truly drunk, walking slowly and carefully as the ground lurched and spun beneath him. He summoned the presence of mind to listen for the streetcar, which came like a bullet at night; just last year it ran down a drunk coming from some bar further up the road. "That's some messy shit," he announced, and laughed to himself. The United Cab offices were just a few blocks away. If he hurried he could beat the rain.

Halfway there he found Ivy, rooting lazily through a trash can.

She was a cute little thing who'd shown up in town last year after fleeing some private doom in Georgia; she was forty years younger than Beltrane, but hoped lived large in him. They got along pretty well—she got along well with most men, really—and it was always nice to spend time with a pretty girl. He waved at her. "Ivy! Hey, girl!"

She looked up at him, her face empty. "'S'up, 'Trane. What you doin?" She straightened and tossed a crumpled wrapper back into the can.

"I'm goin to bed, girl. It's late!"

She appraised him for a moment, then smiled. "You fucked up!"

He laughed, like a little boy caught in some foolishness.

She saw the bag he still clutched in his hand. "I ain't had nothing to eat, 'Trane. I'm starving."

He held the bag aloft, like the head of a slain enemy. "I got some food for ya right here."

She held out a hand and offered him her best smile. It lit up all that alcohol in him. It set him on fire. "Well give it over then," she said.

"You must think I'm crazy. Come on back with me, to my place."

"Shit. That old cab?"

Beltrane turned and walked in that direction, listening to her footsteps as she trotted to catch up. The booze in him caused the earth to move in slow, steady waves, and the lights to bleed into the cloudy night. A cold wind had kicked up, and the buildings swooned on their foundations. Together they trekked the short distance to United Cab.

He found himself, as always, stealing glances at her: though she was gaunt from deprivation, she seemed to have an aura of carved nobility about her, a hard beauty distinct from circumstance or prospect. She was young enough, too, that she still harbored some resilient optimism about the world, as though it might yield some good for her yet. And who knows, he thought. Maybe it would.

The first hard drops of rain fell as they reached the cab. It had died where it was last parked, two years ago. It sagged earthward, its tires long deflated and its shocks long spent, so that the chassis nearly scraped the ground as Beltrane opened the door and climbed in. It smelled like fried food and sweat, and he rubbed the old air freshener hanging from the rearview in some wild hope he could coax a little life from it yet. The front seats had been taken out, giving them room to stretch their legs. The car was packed with blankets, old newspapers, and skin magazines. Ivy stared in after him, wrinkling her nose.

"This is it, baby," he said.

"It stinks in here!"

"It ain't that bad. You get used to it." He leaned against the seatback, stretching his legs to the front. He hooked one arm up over the backseat and invited her to lean into him. She paused, still halfway through the door, on her hands and knees.

"I ain't fuckin you, 'Trane. You too damn old."

"Shit, girl." He tried to pretend he wasn't disappointed. "Get your silly ass in here and have some food."

She climbed in, and he opened the bag for her. The shrimp retained a lingering heat from the microwave at the Pub, and they dug in. Afterwards, with warm food alight in their bellies and the rain hammering on the roof, she eased back against the seat and settled into the crook of his arm at last, resting her head on his shoulder. Beltrane gave her a light squeeze, realizing with a kind of dismay that any sexual urge had left him, that the feeling he harbored for her now was something altogether different, altogether better.

"I don't know nothing about you, 'Trane," she said quietly. "You don't talk very much."

"What you mean? I'm always talking!"

"Yeah, but you don't really talk, you know? Like, you got any family around?"

"Well," he said, his voice trailing. "Somewhere. I got a little girl somewhere."

She lifted her head and looked at him. "For real?"

He just nodded. Something about this conversation felt wrong, but he couldn't figure out what it was. The rain was coming down so hard it was difficult to focus. "I ain't seen her in a long time. She got married and went away."

"She just abandon you? That's fucked up, 'Trane."

"I wasn't like this then. Things was different." Sorrow crested and broke in his chest. "She got to live her life. She had to go."

"You ever think about leaving too? Maybe you could go to where she live."

"Hell no, girl. This is my home. This is everything I know."

"It's just a place, 'Trane. You can change a place easy."

He didn't want to think about that. "Anyway," he said, "she forgot me by now."

Ivy was quiet for a time, and Beltrane let himself be lulled by the drumbeat over their heads. Then she said, "I bet she ain't forgot you." She adjusted her position to get comfortable, putting her head back on his shoulder. "I bet she still love her daddy."

They stopped talking, and eventually she drifted off to sleep. He kissed her gently on her forehead, listening to the storm surrounding the car. The air was chilly, but their bodies were warm against each other. Outside was thrashing darkness, and rain.


Beltrane awoke with a fearful convulsion. The car was filling with water. It was pouring from Ivy, from her eyes and her mouth, from the pores of her skin, in a black torrent, lifting the stored papers and the garbage around them in swirling eddies, rising rapidly over their legs and on up to their waists. The water was appallingly cold; he lost all feeling where it covered him. He put his hands over Ivy's face to staunch the flow, without effect. Her head lolled beside him, her face discolored and grotesquely swollen.

He was going to drown. The idea came to him with a kind of alien majesty; he was overcome with awe and horror.

He pushed against the car door, but it wouldn't open. Beyond the window, the night moved with a murderous will. It lifted the city by its roots and shook it in its teeth. The water had nearly reached the ceiling, and he had to arch his back painfully to keep his face above it. Ivy had already slipped beneath the surface, her lamplit eyes shining like cave fish.

All thought left him: his whole energy was channeled into a scrabbling need to escape. He slammed his body repeatedly into the car door. He pounded the glass with his fists.

Beltrane awakens to pain. His limbs are wracked with it, his elbow especially. He opens his eyes and sees the pavement of the alley. Climbing to his feet takes several minutes. Morning is near: through the mouth of the alley the streetlights glow dimly against a sky breaking slowly into light. There is no traffic, and the salty smell of the bay is strong. The earth has cooled in the night, and the heat's return is still a few hours away.

He takes a step toward the street, then stops, sensing something behind him. He turns around.

A small city has sprouted from the ground in the night, where he'd been sleeping, surrounded by blowing detritus and stagnant filth. It spreads across the puddle-strewn pavement and grows up the side of the wall, twinkling in the deep blue hours of the morning, like some gorgeous fungus, awash in a blustery evening rain. It exudes a sweet, necrotic stink. He's transfixed by it, and the distant wails he hears rising from it are a brutal, beautiful lullaby.

He walks away from it.

When he gets to the street, he turns left, heading down to the small harbor. The door to the church is closed when he passes it, and the lights are off inside. There's no indication of any life there. Soon he passes the shelter, and there are people he recognizes socializing by its front door; but he doesn't know their names, and they don't know his. They don't acknowledge him as he walks by. He passes a little restaurant, the smell of coffee and griddle-cooked sausage hanging in front of it like a cloud. The long white masts of the sailboats are peering over the tops of buildings. He rounds a corner and he is there.

The water of the bay glimmers with bright shards of light as the sun climbs. The boats jostle gently in their berths. A pelican perches on a short pier, wings spread like hanging laundry. He follows a sidewalk along the waterfront until he finds a payphone with a dial tone. He presses zero, and waits.

"I wanna make a collect call," he says, fishing the slip of paper Davis gave him out of his pocket and reciting the number.

He waits for the automated tone, and announces himself. "It's Henry. It's your dad."

A machine says, "Please hold while we connect your call."

Leaning over the small concrete barrier, he can see the shape of himself in the water. His reflection is broken up by the water's movement. Small pieces of himself clash and separate. He thinks that if he waits here long enough the water will calm, and his face will resolve into something familiar.

# The Good Husband

*The water makes her nightgown diaphanous, like the* ghost of something, and she is naked underneath. Her breasts are full, her nipples large and pale, and her soft stomach, where he once loved to rest his head as he ran his hand through the soft tangle of hair between her legs, is stretched with the marks of age. He sits on the lid of the toilet, feeling a removed horror as his cock stirs beneath his robe. Her eyes are flat and shiny as dimes and she doesn't blink as the water splashes over her face. Wispy clouds of blood drift through the water, obscuring his view of her. An empty prescription bottle lies beside the tub, a few bright pills scattered like candy on the floor.

He was not meant to see this, and he feels a minor spasm of guilt, as though he has caught her at something shameful and private. This woman with whom he had once shared all the shabby secrets of his life. The slice in her forearm is an open curtain, blood flowing out in billowing dark banners.

"You're going to be okay, Katie," he says. He has not called her Katie in ten years. He makes no move to save her.


Sean shifted his legs out of bed and pressed his bare feet onto the hardwood floor; it was cold, and his nerves jumped. A spike of life. A sign of movement in the blood. He sat there for a moment, his eyes closed, and concentrated on that. He slid his feet into his slippers and willed himself into a standing position.

He walked naked across the bedroom and fetched his robe from the closet. He threw it around himself and tied it closed. He walked by the vanity, with its alchemies of perfumes and eyeshadows, ignoring the mirror, and left the bedroom. Down the hallway, past the closed bathroom door with light still bleeding from underneath, descending the stairs to the sunlit order of his home.

He was alert to each contraction of muscle, to each creak of bone and ligament. To the pressure of the floor against the soles of his feet, to the slide of the bannister's polished wood against the soft white flesh of his hand.

His mind skated across the frozen surface of each moment. He pushed it along, he pushed it along.


They'd been married twenty-one years, and Katie had tried to kill herself four times in that span. Three times in the last year and a half. Last night, she'd finally gotten it right.

The night had started out wonderfully. They dressed up, went out for dinner, had fun for the first time in recent memory. He bought her flowers, and they walked downtown after dinner and admired the lights and the easy flow of life. He took her to a chocolate shop. Her face was radiant, and a picture of her that final night was locked into his memory: the silver in her hair shining in the reflected light of an overhead lamp, her cheeks rounded into a smile, the soft weight of life turning her body beautiful and inviting, like a blanket, or a hearth. She looked like the girl she used to be. He'd started to believe that with patience and fortitude they could keep at bay the despair that had been seeping into her from some unknown, subterranean hell, flowing around the barricades of antidepressants and anxiety pills, filling her brain with cold water.

When they got home they opened up another bottle and took it to the bedroom. And somehow, they started talking about Heather, who had gone away to college and had recently informed them that she did not want to come home for spring break. It wasn't that she wanted to go anywhere special; she wanted to stay at the dorm, which would be nearly emptied of people, and read, or work, or fuck her new boyfriend if she had one, or whatever it was college girls wanted to do when they didn't want to come home to their parents.

It worked away at Kate like a worm, burrowing tunnels in her gut. She viewed Sean's acceptance of Heather's decision as callous indifference. When the subject came up again that night, he knew the mood was destroyed.

He resented her for it. For spoiling, once again and with what seemed a frivolous cause, the peace and happiness he was trying so hard to give her. If only she would take it. If only she would believe in it. Like she used to do, before her brain turned against her, and against them all.

They drank the bottle even as the despair settled over her. They ended the night sitting on the edge of the bed, she wearing her sexy nightgown, her breasts mostly exposed and moon-pale in the light, weeping soundlessly, a little furrow between her eyebrows but otherwise without affect, and the light sheen of tears which flowed and flowed, as though a foundation had cracked; and he in the red robe she'd bought him for Christmas, his arm around her, trying once again to reason her away from a precipice which reason did not know.

Eventually he lay back and put his arm over his eyes, frustrated and angry. And then he fell asleep.

He awoke sometime later to the sound of splashing water. It should have been too small a sound to reach him, but it did anyway, worming its way into the black and pulling him to the surface. When he discovered that he was alone in the bedroom, and sensed the deepness of the hour, he walked to the bathroom, where the noise came from, without urgency and with a full knowledge of what he would find.

She spasmed every few seconds, as though something in the body, separate from the mind, fought against this.

He sat down on the toilet, watching her. Later he would examine this moment and try to gauge what he had been feeling. It would seem important to take some measure of himself, to find out what kind of man he really was.

He would come to the conclusion that he'd felt tired. It was as though his blood had turned to lead. He knew the procedure he was meant to follow here; he'd done it before. Already his muscles tightened to abide by the routine, signals blew across his nerves like a brushfire: rush to the tub, waste a crucial moment in simple denial brushing the hair from her face and cradling her head in his warm hands. Hook his arms underneath her body and lift her heavily from the water. Carry her, streaming blood and water, to the bed. Call 911. Wait. Wait. Wait. Ride with her, and sit unmoving in the waiting room as they pump her stomach and fill her with a stranger's blood. Answer questions. Does she take drugs. Do you. Were you fighting. Sir, a social worker will be by to talk to you. Sir, you have to fill out these forms. Sir, your wife is broken, and you are, too.

And then wait some more as she convalesces in the psych ward. Visit her, try not to cry in front of her as you see her haunting that corridor with the rest of the damned, dwelling like a fading thought in her assigned room.

Bring this pale thing home. This husk, this hollowed vessel. Nurse her to a false health. Listen to her apologize, and accept her apologies. Profess your reinvigorated love. Fuck her with the urgency of pity and mortality and fear, which you both have come to know and to rely on the way you once relied on love and physical desire.

*If* they could save her.

And if, having saved her, they decided to let her come home at all.

*She will never be happy.*

The thought came to him with the force of a revelation. It was as though God spoke a judgment, and he recognized its truth as though it had been with them all along, the buzzard companion of their late marriage. Some people, he thought, are just incapable of happiness. Maybe it was because of some ancient trauma, or maybe it was just a bad equation in the brain. Kate's reasons were mysterious to him, a fact which appalled him after so many years of intimacy. If he pulled her from the water now, he would just be welcoming her back to hell.

With a flutter of some obscure emotion—some solution of terror and relief—he closed the door on her. He went back to bed and, after a few sleeping pills of his own, fell into a black sleep. He dreamed of silence.


In the kitchen, light streamed in through the bay window. It was a big kitchen, with a stand-alone chopping table, wide crumb-flecked counters, ranks of silver knives agleam in the morning sun. Dirty dishes were stacked in the sink and on the counter beside it. The trash hadn't been taken out on time, and its odor was a dull oppression. The kitchen had once been the pride of their home. It seemed to have decayed without his noticing.

A small breakfast nook accommodated a kitchen table in a narrow passage joining the kitchen to the dining room. It still bore the scars and markings of the younger Heather's attentions: divots in the wood where she once tested the effectiveness of a butter knife, a spray of red paint left there during one of her innumerable art projects, and the word "kichen" gouged into the side of the table with a ballpoint pen, years ago, when she thought everything should carry its name. It had become an inadvertent shrine to her childhood, and, since she'd left, Kate had shifted their morning coffee to the larger and less welcoming dining room table in the adjoining room. The little breakfast nook had been surrendered to the natural entropy of a household, becoming little more than a receptacle for car keys and unopened mail.

Sean filled the French press with coffee grounds and put the water on to boil.

For a few crucial minutes he had nothing to do, and a ferocious panic began to chew at the border of his thoughts. He felt a weight descending from the floor above him. An unseen face. He thought for a moment that he could hear her footsteps. He thought for a moment that nothing had changed.

He was looking through the bay window to the garden out front, which had ceded vital ground to weeds and ivy. Across the street he watched his neighbor's grandkids tear around the corner of their house like crazed orangutans: ill-built yet strangely graceful, spurred by an unknowable animal purpose. It was Saturday; though winter still lingered at night, spring was warming the daylight hours.

Apparently it was a beautiful day.

The kettle began to hiss, and he returned to his rote tasks. Pour the water into the press. Stir the contents. Fit the lid into place and wait for the contents to steep. He fetched a single mug from the cabinet and waited at the counter.

He heard something move behind him, the soft pad of a foot on the linoleum, the staccato tap of dripping water. He turned and saw his wife standing at the kitchen's threshold, the nightgown still soaked through and clinging intimately to her body, streams of water running from the gown and from her hair, which hung in a thick black sheet, and pooling brightly around her.

A sound escaped him, a syllable shot like a hard pellet, high-pitched and meaningless. His body jerked as though yanked by some invisible cord and the coffee mug launched from his hand and shattered on the floor between them. Kate sat down in the nook; the first time she'd sat there in almost a year. She did not look at him, or react to the smashed mug. Water pit-patted from her hair and her clothes, onto the table. "Where's mine?" she said.

"Kate? What?"

"Where's my coffee? I want coffee. I'm cold. You forgot mine."

He worked his jaw, trying to coax some sound. Finally he said, "All right." His voice was weak and undirected. "All right," he said again. He opened the cabinet and fetched two mugs.

She'd had a bad dream. It was the only thing that made sense. She was cold and wet and something in her brain tried to arrange it into a logical shape. She remembered seeing Sean's face through a veil of water. Watching it recede from her. She felt a buckle of nausea at the memory. She took a drink from the coffee and felt the heat course through her body. It only made her feel worse.

She rubbed her hands at her temples.

"Why am I all wet?" she said. "I don't feel right. Something's wrong with me. Something's really wrong."

Sean guided her upstairs. She reacted to his gentle guidance, but did not seem to be acting under any will of her own; except when he tried to steer her into the bathroom. She resisted then, turning to stone in the hallway. "No," she said. Her eyes were hard and bright with fear. She turned her head away from the door. He took her wrist to pull her, but she resisted. His fingers inadvertently slid over the incision there, and he jerked his hand away.

"Honey. We need to fix you up."

"No."

He relented, taking her to the bedroom instead, where he removed her wet nightgown. It struck him that he had not seen her like this, standing naked in the plain light of day, for a long time. They had been married for over twenty years, and they'd lost interest in each other's bodies long ago. When she was naked in front of him now he barely noticed. Her body was part of the furniture of their marriage, utilized but ignored, with occasional benign observations from them both about its declining condition.

In a sudden resurgence of his feelings of the previous night, he became achingly aware of her physicality. She was so pale: the marble white of statues, or of sunbleached bones. Her flesh hung loosely on her body, the extra weight suddenly obvious, as though she had no muscle tone remaining at all. Her breasts, her stomach, her unshaven hair: the human frailty of her, the beauty of a lived-in body, which he knew was reflected in his own body, called up a surge of tenderness and sympathy.

"Let's put some clothes on," he said, turning away from her.

He helped her step into her underwear, found a bra and hooked her into it. He found some comfortable, loose-fitting clothes for her, things he knew she liked to wear when she had nowhere special to go. It was not until he was fitting her old college reunion T-shirt over her head that he allowed himself to look at her wrist for the first time, and the sight of it made him step back and clasp a hand over his mouth.

Her left arm bore a long incision from wrist to elbow. The flesh puckered like lips, and as she bent her arm into the shirt he was afforded a glimpse at the awful depth of the wound. It was easily deep enough to affect its purpose, and as bloodless as the belly of a gutted fish.

"Katie," he said, and brought her wrist to his lips. "What's happening to you?" He pressed his fingers to her cheek; they were cool, and limp. "Are you okay?" It was the stupidest question of his life. But he didn't know what else to ask. "Katie?"

She turned her face to him, and after a few moments he could see her eyes begin to focus on him, as though she had to travel a terrible span to find him there. "I don't know," she said. "Something doesn't feel right."

"Do you want to lie down?"

"I guess."

He eased her toward her side of the bed, which was smooth and untroubled: she had slept underwater last night; not here. He laid her there like folded laundry.

He sat beside her as she drifted off. Her eyes remained open, but she seemed gone; she seemed truly dead. Maybe, this time, she was.

Does she remember? he thought. Does she remember that I left her? He stretched himself out beside her and ran his hand through her hair, repetitively, a kind of prayer.

Oh my God, he thought, what have I done? What is happening to me?


Eventually she wanted to go outside. Not at first, because she was scared, and the world did not make any sense to her. The air tasted strange on her tongue, and her body felt heavy and foreign—she felt very much like a thought wrapped in meat. She spent a few days drifting through the house in a lethargic haze, trying to shed the feeling of unease which she had woken with the morning after her bath, and which had stayed rooted in her throat and in her gut the whole time since. Sean came and went to work. He was solicitous and kind; he was always extra attentive after she tried to kill herself, though; and although she welcomed the attention, she had learned to distrust it. She knew it would fade, once the nearness of death receded.

She watched the world through the window. It was like a moving picture in a frame; the details did not change, but the wind blew through the grass and the trees and the neighbors came and went in their cars, giving the scene the illusion of reality. Once, in the late afternoon before Sean came home, she was seen. The older man who lived across the street, whose cat she fed when he went out of town and who was a friend to them both, caught sight of her as he stepped out of his car and waved. She only stared back. After a moment, the man turned from her and disappeared into his own house.

The outside world was a dream of another place. She found herself wondering if she would fit better there.

On the evening of the third day, while they were sitting at dinner—something wretched and cooling that Sean had picked up on his way home—she told him.

"I want to go outside."

Sean kept eating as though he didn't hear her.

This was not new. He'd been behaving with an almost manic enthusiasm around her, as though he could convince her that their lives were unskewed and smooth through sheer force of will. But he would not look at her face; when he looked at her at all, he would focus on her cheek, or her shoulder, or her hairline. He would almost look at her. But not quite.

"I don't know if that's a good idea," he said at last. He ate ferociously, forking more into his mouth before he was finished with the last bite.

"Why not?"

He paused, his eyes lifting briefly to the salt and pepper shakers in the middle of the table. "You still don't seem . . . I don't know. Yourself."

"And what would that be like?" She had not touched her food, except to prod it the way a child pokes a stick at roadkill. It cooled on the plate in front of her, congealing cheese and oils. It made her sick.

His mood swung abruptly into something more withdrawn and depressed; she could watch his face and see it happen. This made her feel better. This was more like the man she had known for the past several years of their marriage.

"Am I a prisoner here?"

He finally looked at her, shocked and hurt. "What? How could you even say that?"

She said nothing. She just held his gaze.

He looked terrified. "I'm just worried about you, babe. You don't—you're not—"

"You mean this?" She raised her left arm and slipped her finger into the open wound. It was as clean and bloodless as rubber.

Sean lowered his face. "Don't do that."

"If you're really worried about me, why don't you take me to the hospital? Why didn't you call an ambulance? I've been sleeping so much the past few days. But you just go on to work like everything's fine."

"Everything *is* fine."

"I don't think so."

He was looking out the window now. The sun was going down and the light was thick and golden. Their garden was flowering, and a light dusting of pollen coated the left side of their car in the driveway. Sean's eyes were unblinking and reflective as water. He stared at it all. "There's nothing wrong with you," he said.

Silence filled the space between them as they each sat still in their own thoughts. The refrigerator hummed to life. Katie finally pushed herself away from the table and headed toward the door, scooping up the car keys on her way.

"I'm going out," she said.

"Where?" His voice was thick with resignation.

"Maybe to the store. Maybe nowhere. I'll be back soon."

He moved to stand. "I'll come with."

"No thanks," she said, and he slumped back into his chair.

Once, she would have felt guilty for that. She would have chastised herself for failing to take into account his wishes or his fears, for failing to protect his fragile ego. He was a delicate man, though he did not know it, and she had long considered it part of her obligation to the marriage to accommodate that frailty of spirit.

But she felt a separation from that now. And from him, too, though she remembered loving him once. If anything inspired guilt, it was that she could not seem to find that love anymore. He was a good man, and deserved to be loved. She wondered if the ghost of a feeling could substitute for the feeling itself.

But worse than all of that was the separation she felt from herself. She'd felt like a passenger in her own body the last three days, the pilot of some arcane machine. She watched from a remove as the flesh of her hand tightened around the doorknob and rotated it clockwise, setting into motion the mechanical process which would free the door from its jamb and allow it to swing open, freeing her avenue of escape. The flesh was a mechanism, too, a contracting of muscle and ligament, an exertion of pull.

*There's nothing wrong with you,* he'd said.

She opened the door.

The light was like ground glass in her eyes. It was the most astonishing pain she had ever experienced. She screamed, dropped to the floor, and curled into herself. Very distantly she heard something heavy fall over, followed by crashing footsteps which thrummed the floor beneath her head, and then the door slammed shut. Her husband's hands fell on her and she twisted away from them. The light was a paste on her eyes; she couldn't seem to claw it off of them. It bled into her skull and filled it like a poisonous radiation. She lurched to her feet, shouldering Sean aside, and ran away from the door and into the living room, where she tripped over the carpet and landed hard on her side. Her husband's hysterical voice followed her, a blast of panic. She pushed her body forward with her feet, wedged her face into the space beneath the couch, the cool darkness there, and tried to claw away the astounding misery of the light.


That night she would not come to bed. They'd been sleeping beside each other since the suicide, though he was careful to keep space between them, and had taken to wearing pajamas to bed. She slept fitfully at night, seeming to rest better in the daylight, and this troubled his own sleep, too. She would be as still as stone and then struggle elaborately with the sheets for a few moments before settling into stillness again, like a drowning woman. He turned his head toward the wall when this happened. And then he would remember that he'd turned away from her that night, too. And he would stay awake into the small hours, feeling her struggle, knowing that he'd missed his chance to help her.

The incident at the door had galvanized him, though. Her pain was terrifying in its intensity, and it was his fault. He would not let his guilt or his shame prevent him from doing whatever was necessary to keep her safe and comfortable from now on. Love still lived in him, like some hibernating serpent, and it stirred now. It tasted the air with its tongue.

It took her some time to calm down. He fixed her a martini and brought it to her, watched her sip it disinterestedly as she sat on the couch and stared at the floor, her voice breaking every once in a while in small hiccups of distress. Long nail marks scored her skin; her right eye seemed jostled in its orbit, angled fractionally lower than the other. He had drawn the curtains and pulled the blinds, though by now the sun had sunk and the world outside was blue and cool. He turned off all but a few lights in the house, filling it with shadows. Whether it was this, or the vodka, or something else that did it, she finally settled into a fraught silence.

He eased himself onto the couch beside her, and he took her chin in his fingers and turned her face toward him. An echo of his thought from the night of the suicide passed through his mind: *She will never get better.*

He felt his throat constrict, and heat gathered in his eyes.

"Katie?" He put his hand on her knee. "Talk to me, babe."

She was motionless. He didn't even know if she could hear him.

"Are you all right? Are you in any pain?"

After a long moment, she said, "It was in my head."

"What was?"

"The light. I couldn't get it out."

He nodded, trying to figure out what this meant. "Well. It's dark now."

"Thank you," she said.

This small gratitude caused an absurd swelling in his heart, and he cupped her cheek in his hand. "Oh baby," he said. "I was so scared. I don't know what's going on. I don't know what to do for you."

She put her own hand over his, and pressed her cheek into his palm. Her eyes remained unfocused though, one askew, almost as if this was a learned reaction. A muscle memory. Nothing more.

"I don't understand anything anymore," she said. "Everything is strange."

"I know."

She seemed to consider something for a moment. "I should go somewhere else," she said.

"No," Sean said. A violence moved inside him, the idea of her leaving calling forth an animal fury, aimless and electric. "No, Katie. You don't understand. They'll take you away from me. If I take you somewhere, if I take you to see someone, they will not let you come back. You just stay here. You're safe here. We'll keep things dark, like you like it. We'll do whatever it takes. Okay?"

She looked at him. The lamplight from the other room reflected from her irises, giving them a creamy whiteness that looked warm and soft, incongruous in her torn face, like saucers of milk left out after the end of the world. "Why?"

The question shamed him. "Because I love you, Katie. Jesus Christ. You're my wife. I love you."

"I love you, too," she said, and like pressing her cheek into his hand, this response seemed an automatic action. A programmed response. He ignored this, though, and chose to accept what she said as truth—perhaps because this was the first time she'd said it to him since the suicide, when her body had stopped behaving in the way it was meant to and conformed to a new logic, a biology he did not recognize and could not understand and which made a mystery of her again. It had been so long since she'd been a mystery to him. He knew every detail of her life, every dull complaint and every stillborn dream, and she knew his; but now he knew nothing. Every nerve ending in his body was turned in her direction, like flowers bending to the sun.

Or perhaps he only accepted it because the light was soft, and it exalted her.

His free hand found her breast. She did not react in any way. He squeezed it gently in his hand, his thumb rolling over her nipple, still soft under her shirt. She allowed all of this, but her face was empty. He pulled away from her. "Let's go upstairs," he said.

He rose and, taking her hand, moved to help her to her feet. She resisted.

"Katie, come on. Let's go to bed."

"I don't want to."

"But don't you . . ." He took her hand and pressed it against his cock, stiff in his pants. "Can you feel that? Can you feel what you do to me?"

"I don't want to go upstairs. The light will come in in the morning. I want to sleep in the cellar."

He released her hand, and it dropped to her side. He thought for a minute. The cellar was used for storage, and was in a chaotic state. But there was room for a mattress down there, and tomorrow he could move things around, make some arrangements, and make it livable. It did not occur to him to argue with her. This was part of the mystery, and it excited him. He was like a high school boy with a mad new crush, prepared to go to any length.

"Okay," he said. "Give me a few minutes. I'll make it nice for you."

He left her sitting in the dark, his heart pounding, red and strong.

He fucked her with the ardor one brings to a new lover, sliding into the surprising coolness of her, tangling his fingers into her hair and biting her neck, her chin, her ears. He wanted to devour her, to breathe her like an atmosphere. He hadn't been so hard in years; his body moved like a piston, and he felt he could go on for hours. He slid his arms beneath her and held her shoulders from behind as he powered into her, the mattress silent beneath them, the darkness of the cellar as gentle and welcoming as a mother's heart. At first she wrapped her legs around his back, put her arms over his shoulders, but by the time he finished she had abandoned the pretense and simply lay still beneath him, one eye focused on the underbeams of the ceiling, one eye peering into the black.

Afterwards he lay beside her, staring up at the underside of his house. The cellar was cold and stank of mildew. The piled clutter of a long and settled life loomed around them in mounted stacks, tall black shadows which gazed down upon them like some alien congress. The mattress beneath them came from their own bed; he'd resolved to sleep down here with her, if this was where she wanted to be. Three candles were gathered in a little group by their heads, not because he thought it would be romantic—though he felt that it was—but because he had no idea where the outlets were down here to set up a lamp, and he didn't want to risk upsetting her by turning on the bare bulb in the ceiling. The candle-light didn't seem to bother her at all, though; maybe it was just the sun.

He turned his head on the pillow to look at her, and ran his hand along the length of her body. It was cool to the touch, cool inside and out.

"This other light doesn't bother you, does it, babe?"

She turned her head too, slowly, and looked at him. Her wounds cast garish shadows across her face in the candlelight. "Hmm?"

"The light?"

". . . Oh, I know you," she said, something like relief in her voice. "You're the man who left me in the water."

Something cold flowed through his body. "What?"

She settled back against the mattress, closing her eyes and pull-ing the sheet up to her chin. She seemed very content. "I couldn't remember you for a minute, but then I did."

"Do you remember that night?"

"What night?"

". . . You said I'm the man who left you in the water."

"I looked up and I saw you. I was scared of something. I thought you were going to help, but then you went away. What was I scared of? Do you know?"

He shook his head, but her eyes were closed and she couldn't see him. "No," he said at last.

"I wish I could remember."

She climbed off the mattress, leaving the man to sleep. He snored loudly, and this made her think of machines again. His was a clumsy one, loud and rattling, and its inefficiency irritated her. It was corpulent and heavy, uncared for, and breaking down. She decided at that moment that she would not let it touch her again.

She slipped her nightgown on over her head and walked upstairs. Cautiously, she opened the door at the top and peered into the ground floor of the house. It was welcomingly dark. Crossing the living room floor and parting the curtains, she saw that night had fallen.

Within moments she was outside, walking briskly along the sidewalk, crackling with an energy she hadn't felt in as long as she could remember. The houses on either side of the street were high-shouldered monsters, their windows as black and silent as the sky above her. The yawn of space opened just beneath the surface of her thoughts with a gorgeous silence. She wanted to sink into it, but she couldn't figure out how. Each darkened building held the promise of tombs, and she had to remind herself that she could not go inside them because people lived there, those churning, squirting biologies, and that the quietude she sought would be found somewhere else.

She remembered a place she could go, though. She quickened her pace, her nightgown—the one she had worn that night, when the man had left her in the water, now clean and white—almost ephemeral in the chilly air and trailing behind her like a ghostly film. The narrow suburban road crested a hill a few hundred feet ahead, and beyond it breached a low dome of light. The city, burning light against the darkness.

Something lay on the sidewalk in front of her, and she slowed as she approached. It was a robin, its middle torn open, its guts eaten away. A curtain of ants flowed inside it and led away from it in a meandering trail into the grass. She picked it up and cradled it close to her face. The ants seethed, spreading through its feathers, over her hand, down her arm. She ignored them.

The bird's eyes were glassy and black, like tiny onyx stones. Its beak was open, and in it she could see the soft red muscle of its tongue. Something moved and glistened in the back of its throat.

She continued on, holding the robin at her side. She didn't feel the ants crawling up her arm, onto her neck, into her hair. The bird was a miracle of beauty.

The suburbs stopped at the highway, like an island against the sea. She turned east, the city lights brighter now at her right, and continued walking. The sidewalk roughened as she continued along, broken in places, seasoned with stones and broken glass. She was oblivious to it all. Traffic was light but not incidental, and the rush of cars blowing by lifted her hair and flattened the nightgown against her body. Someone leaned on the horn as he drove past, whooping through an open window.

The clamor of the highway, the stink of oil and gasoline, the buffeting rush of traffic, all served to deepen her sense of displacement. The world was a bewildering, foreign place, the light a low-grade burn and a stain on the air, the rushing cars on the highway a row of gnashing teeth.

But ahead, finally, opening in long, silent acres to her left, was the cemetery.

It was gated and locked, but finding a tree to get over the wall was no difficulty. She scraped her skin on the bark and then on the stone, and she tore her nightgown, but that was of no consequence. She tumbled gracelessly to the ground, like a dropped sack, and felt a sharp snap in her right ankle. When she tried to walk, the ankle rolled beneath her and she fell.

Meat, getting in the way.

Disgusted by this, she used the wall to pull herself to a standing position. She found that if she let the foot just roll to the side and walked on the ankle itself, she could make a clumsy progress.

Clouds obscured the sky, and the cemetery stretched over a rolling landscape, bristling with headstones and plaques, monuments and crypts, like a scattering of teeth. It was old; many generations were buried here. The sound of the highway, muffled by the wall, faded entirely from her awareness. She stood amidst the graves and let their silence fill her.

The flutter of unease that she'd felt since waking after the suicide abated. The sense of disconnection was gone. Her heart was a still lake. Nothing in her moved. She wanted to cry from relief.

Still holding the dead robin in her hand, she lurched more deeply into the cemetery.

She found a hollow between the stones, a trough between the stilled waves of earth, where no burial was marked. She eased herself to the ground and curled up in the grass. The clouds were heavy and thick, the air was cold. She closed her eyes and felt the cooling of her brain.

Sounds rose from the earth. New sounds: cobwebs of exhalations, pauses of the heart, the monastic work of the worms translating flesh to soil, the slow crawl of rock. There was another kind of industry, somewhere beneath her. Another kind of machine.

It was new knowledge, and she felt the root of a purpose. She set the robin aside and tore grass away, dug her nails into the dark soil, pushed through. She scooped aside handfuls of dirt. At some point in her labors she became aware of something awaiting her beneath the earth. Moving silences, the cloudy breaths of the moon, magnificent shapes unrecognizable to her novice intelligence, like strange old galleons of the sea.

And then, something awful. A rough bark, a perverse intrusion into this quiet celebration, a rape of the silence.

Her husband's voice.

She was alone again, and she felt his rough hands upon her.

*♥*

It had been nothing more than instinct which guided him to her, finally. He panicked when he awoke to her missing, careened through the house, shouted like a fool in his front yard until lights began to pop on in the neighbors' houses. Afraid that they would offer to help, or call the police for him, he got into the car and started driving. He criss-crossed the neighborhood to no avail, until finally it occurred to him that she might go to the cemetery. That she might, in some fit of delirium, decide that she belonged there.

The thought tore at him. The guilt over leaving her to die in the bathtub threatened to crack his ribs. It was too big to contain.

He scaled the cemetery wall and called until he found her, a small white form in a sea of graves and dark grass, huddled and scared, clawing desperately in the dirt. Her ankle was broken and hung at a sickening angle.

He pulled her up by her shoulders and wrapped his arms around her, hugged her tightly against him.

"Oh Katie, oh baby," he said. "It's okay. It's okay. I've got you. You scared me so bad. You're going to be okay."

An ant emerged from her hairline and idled on her forehead. Another crawled out of her nose. He brushed them furiously away.


She returned to the cellar. He spent a few days getting it into some kind of order, moving precarious stacks into smaller and sturdier piles, and giving her some room to move around in. While she slept in the daytime he brought down the television set and its stand, a lamp, and a small box where he kept the books she had once liked to read. He left the mattress on the floor but changed the sheets regularly. When he was not at work he spent all his time down there with her, though he had taken to sleeping upstairs so that he could lock her in when she was most likely to try to wander.

"I can't risk you getting lost again," he told her. "It would kill me." Then he closed the door and turned the lock. She heard his steps tread the floor above her.

She had taken the dead robin and nailed it to one of the support beams beside the mattress. It was the only beautiful thing in the room, and it calmed her to look at it.

Her foot was more trouble than it was worth so she wrenched it off and tossed it into the corner.

"That was Heather," Sean said, closing the cellar door and tromping down the stairs. He sat beside her on the mattress and put his arm around her shoulders. She did not lean into him the way she used to do, so he gave her a little pull until it seemed like she was.

When he'd noticed her missing foot the other night he'd quietly gone back upstairs and dry heaved over the sink. Then he came back down, searched until he located it in a corner, and took it outside to bury it. The crucified bird had not bothered him initially, but over the days it had gathered company: two mice, three cockroaches, a wasp, some moths. Their dry little bodies were arrayed like art. She had even pulled the bones from one of the mice, fixing them with wood glue onto the post in some arcane hieroglyph.

He was frightened by its alienness. He was frightened because it meant something to her and it was indecipherable to him.

She was watching something on TV with the sound off: men in suits talking to each other across a table. They seemed very earnest.

"She wants to come home for the weekend," he said. "I said it would be okay."

She pulled her gaze from the screen and looked at him. The light from the television made small blue squares in her eyes, which had begun to film over in a creamy haze. It was getting hard to tell that one eye was askew, which made him feel better when he talked to her. "Heather," she said. "I like Heather."

He put his fingers in her hair, hooked a dark lock behind her ear. "Of course you do, baby. You remember her, don't you."

She stared for a moment, then her brow furrowed. "She used to live here."

"That's right. She went to college, and she lives there now. She's our daughter. We love her."

"I forgot."

"And you love me, too."

"Okay."

She looked back at the television. One of the men was standing now, and laughing so hard his face was red. His mouth was wide open. He was going to swallow the world.

"Can you say it?"

"Say what?"

"That you love me. Can you say that to me? Please?"

"I love you."

"Oh baby," he said, and leaned his head against hers, his arm still around her. "Thank you. Thank you. I love you too."

They sat there and watched the silent images. His mind crept ahead to Heather's visit. He wondered what the hell he was going to tell her. She was going to have a hard time with this.


What is the story of our marriage?

He went back to that night again and again. He remembered standing over her, watching her body struggle against the pull of a death she had called upon herself. It is the nature of the body to want to live, and once her mind had shut down her muscles spasmed in the water, splashing blood onto the floor as it fought to save itself.

But her mind, apparently, had not completely shut down after all. She remembered him standing over her. She looked up as the water lapped over her face and saw him staring down at her. She saw him turn and close the door.

What did she see behind his face? Did she believe it was impassive? Did she believe it was unmoved by love? How could he explain that he had done it because he could not bear to watch her suffer anymore?

On the rare occasions that he remembered the other thoughts—the weariness, the dread of the medical routine, and especially the flaring anger he'd felt earlier that same night, when the depression took her and he knew he'd have to steer her through it yet again—he buried them.

That is not the story of our marriage, he thought. The story is that I love her, and that's what guided my actions. As it always has.

He was losing her, though. The change which kindled his interest also pulled her farther and farther away, and he feared that his love for her, and hers for him, would not be enough to tether her to this world.

So he called Heather and told her to come home for spring break. Not for the whole week; he knew that she was an adult now, she had friends, that was fine. But she had family obligations, and her mother was lonely for her, and she should come home for at least the weekend.

Is she sick? Heather asked.

No. She just misses her girl.

Dad, you told me it was okay if I stayed here spring break. You told me you would talk to Mom about it.

I did talk, Heather. She won. Come on home, just for the weekend. Please.

Heather agreed, finally. Her reluctance was palpable, but she would come.

That was step one.

Step two would be coaxing Katie out of the cellar for her arrival. He'd thought that being locked down there at night, and whenever he was out, would have made coming upstairs something to look forward to. He'd been wrong; she showed no signs of wanting to leave the cellar at all, possibly ever again. She had regressed even further, not getting up to walk at all since losing her foot, and forsaking clothing altogether; she crawled palely naked across the floor when she wanted to move anywhere—a want which rarely troubled her mind anymore. She allowed him to wash her when he approached her with soap and warm water, but only because she was passive in this as she had become in all things.

Unless he wanted to touch her with another purpose.

Then she would turn on him with an anger that terrified him. Her eyes were pale as moon rocks. Her breath was cold. And when she turned on him with that fury, he would imagine her breathing that chill into his lungs, stuffing it down into his heart. It terrified him. He would not approach her for sex anymore, though the rejection hurt him more than he would have dreamed.

He decided to woo her. He searched the roads at night, crawling along in his car at under twenty miles an hour, looking for roadkill. The first time he found some, a gut-crushed possum, he brought the carcass into the house and dropped it onto the floor in front of the cellar door, hoping the smell would lure her out. It did not; but he did not sulk, nor did he deprive her of her gift. He opened the door and rolled the animal wreckage down the stairs.

On the night he told her about Heather, he was propelled by romantic impulse to greater heights. He poisoned the cat that lived across the street, the one she loved and watched over when its owner left town, and brought it to her on a pillow; he'd curled it into a semblance of sleep, and laid it at the foot of her mattress. She fixed her flat, pale eyes on it, not acknowledging his presence at all. Slowly she scooped it into her arms, and she held it close to her body. Satisfied, he sat beside her on the bed. He smiled as she got to work.


The floor was packed dirt. It seemed as hard as concrete, but ultimately it was just earth. It could be opened. She bent herself to this task. She found a corner behind some boxes of old china, where her work would not be obvious to the man when he came down to visit, and picked at the ground with a garden spade. It took a long time, but finally she began to make serious progress, upturning the packed ground until she got to the dark soil beneath it, bringing pale earth-worms and slick, black insects to their first, shocked exposure to the upside world. When she got deep enough she abandoned the small spade and used her hands. Her fingernails snapped off like little plastic tabs, and she examined her fingers with a mild curiosity.

Staring at the ruined flesh reminded her of how the man's face would sometimes leak fluid when he came down here, and of his occasional wet cough.

It was all so disgusting.

She took one of the cat's bones from its place on the wall and snapped it in half. The end was sharp and she scraped the flesh from her fingers until hard bone gleamed. Then she went to work again, and was pleased with the difference.


"Hey, Dad." Heather stood in the doorway, her overnight bag slung over her shoulder. Considering how little she wanted to be here, Sean thought she was doing a good job of putting up a positive front.

"Hey, kiddo." He looked over her shoulder and saw that she had parked directly behind his car again, like she always used to do, and like he had asked her not to do a million times. He actually felt a happy nostalgia at the sight of it. He kissed her cheek and took the bag from her shoulder. "Come on in."

She followed him in, rubbing her arms and shuddering. "Jeez, Dad, crank up the AC why don't you."

"Heh, sorry. Your mother likes it cold."

"*Mom?* Since when?"

"Since recently I guess. Listen, why don't you go on up to your room and get changed or whatever. I'll get dinner started."

"Sentimental as always, Dad. I've been in the car all day, and I *really* need a shower. Just call me when you're ready." She brushed past him on her way to the stairs.

"Hey," he said.

She stopped.

He held an arm out. "I'm sorry. Come here."

She did, and he folded his arm around her, drawing her close. He kissed her forehead. "It means a lot that you came."

"I know."

"I'm serious. It matters. Thank you."

"Okay. You're welcome." She returned his hug, and he soaked it in. "So where is she?"

"Downstairs. She'll be up."

She pulled back. "In the *cellar?* Okay, weird."

"She'll be up. Go on now. Get yourself ready."

She shook her head with the muted exasperation of a child long-accustomed to her parents' eccentricities, and mounted the stairs. Sean turned his attention to the kitchen. He'd made some pot roast in the Crock-Pot, and he tilted the lid to give it a look. The warm, heavy smell of it washed over his face, and he took it into his lungs with gratitude. He hadn't prepared anything real to eat in a month, it seemed, living instead off of frozen pizzas and TV dinners. The thought of real food made him lightheaded.

He walked over to the basement door and slid open the lock. He paused briefly, resting his head against the doorjamb. He breathed deeply. Then he cracked it open and poked his head in. A thick, loamy odor rode over him on cool air. There was no light downstairs at all.

"Katie?"

Silence.

"Katie, Heather's here. You remember, we talked about Heather."

His voice did not seem to carry at all on the heavy air. It was like speaking into a cloth.

"She's our daughter." His voice grew small. "You love her, remember?"

He thought he heard something shift down there, a sliding of something. Good, he thought. She remembers.

Heather came downstairs a little later. He waited for her, ladling the pot roast into two bowls. The little breakfast nook was set up for them both. Seeing her, he was struck, as he was so often, by how much like a younger version of Katie she looked. The same roundness in her face, the same way she tended to angle her shoulders when she stood still, even the same bob to her hair. It was as though a young Katie had slipped sideways through a hole in the world and come here to see him again, to see what kind of man he had become. What manner of man she had married.

He lowered his eyes.

I'm a good man, he thought.

"Dad?"

He looked up, blinking his eyes rapidly. "Hey you."

"Why isn't there a mattress on your bed? And why is there a sleeping bag on the floor?"

He shook his head. "What were you doing in our bedroom?"

"The door was wide open. It's kind of hard to miss."

He wasn't expecting this. "It's . . . I've been sleeping on the floor."

She just stared at him. He could see the pain in her face, the old familiar fear. "What's been going on here, Dad? What's she done this time?"

"She uh . . . she's not doing very well, Heather."

He watched tears gather in her eyelids. Then her face darkened and she rubbed them roughly away. "You told me she was fine," she said quietly.

"I didn't want to upset you. I wanted you to come home."

"You didn't want to *upset* me?" Her voice rose into a shout. Her hand clenched at her side, and he watched her wrestle down the anger. It took her a minute.

"I'm sorry, Heather."

She shook her head. She wouldn't look at him. "Whatever. Did she try to kill herself again? She's not even here at all, is she. Is she in the psych ward?"

"No, she's here. And yes, she did."

She turned her back to him and walked into the living room, where she dropped onto the couch and slouched back, her arms crossed over her chest like a child. Sean followed her, pried loose one of her hands and held onto it as he sat beside her.

"She needs us, kiddo."

"I would *never* have come back!" she said, her rage cresting like a sun. "God damn it!"

"Hey! Now listen to me. She needs us."

"She needs to be committed!"

"Stop it. Stop that. I know this is hard."

"Oh do you?" She glared at him, her face red. He had never seen her like this; anger made her face into something ugly and unrecognizable. "*How* do you know, Dad? When did you ever have to deal with it? It was always me! I was the one at home with her. I was the one who had to call the hospital that one time I found her in her own blood and then call you so you could come! I was the one who—" She gave in then, abruptly and catastrophically, like a battlement falling; sobs broke up whatever else she was going to say. She pulled in a shuddering breath and said, "I can't believe you *tricked* me!"

"*Every night!*" Sean hissed, his own large hands wrapped into fists, cudgels on his lap. He saw them there and caught himself. He felt something slide down over his mind. The emotions pulled away, the guilt and the horror and the shame, until he was only looking at someone having a fit. People, it seemed, were always having some kind of breakdown or another. Somebody had to keep it together. Somebody always had to keep it together.

"It was *not* just you. Every night I came home to it. Will she be okay tonight? Will she be normal? Or will she talk about walking in front of a bus? Will she be crying because of something I said, or she thinks I said, last fucking week? Every night. Do you think it all just went away when you went to sleep? Come out of your narcissistic little bubble and realize that the world is bigger than you."

She looked at him, shocked and hurt. Her lower lip was trembling, and the tears came back in force.

"But I always stood by her side. Always." He took her lightly by the arm and stood with her. "Your mother needs us. And we're going to go see her. Right now."

He led her toward the basement door.

What is the story of our family?

He led her down the stairs, into the cool, earthy musk of the basement, the smell of upturned soil a dank bloom in the air. His grip on her arm was firm as he descended one step ahead of her. The light from the kitchen behind them was an ax blade in the darkness, cutting a narrow wedge. It illuminated the corner of the mattress, powdered with a layer of dirt. Beside it, the bottom two feet of the support beam she had nailed the bird to; something new was screwed into place there, but he could intuit from the glistening mass only gristle and hair, a sheet of dried blood beneath it.

"What's going on here? Oh my God, Dad, what's going on?"

"Your mom's in trouble. She needs us."

Heather made a noise and he clamped down harder on her arm.

"Katie?" he said. "Heather's here." His voice did not carry, the words dropping like stones at his feet.

Our family has weathered great upheaval. Our family is bound together by love.

They heard something shift, in the darkness beyond the reach of the light.

"Mom?"

"Katie? Where are you, honey?"

"Dad, what happened to her?"

"Just tell me where you are, sweetheart. We'll come to you."

They reached the bottom of the steps, and as he moved out of the path of the kitchen light it shone more fully on the thing fixed to the post: a gory mass of scrambled flesh, a ragged web of graying black hair. Something moved in the shadows beyond it, small and hunched and pale, its back buckling with each grunted effort, like something caught in the act of love.

Our family will not abandon itself.

Heather stepped backward; her heel caught on the lowest step and she fell onto the stairs.

Sean approached his wife. She labored weakly in the bottom of a small declivity, grave-shaped, worm-spangled, her dull white bones poking through the parchment skin of her back, her spine bending as she burrowed into the earth. Her denuded skull still bore the tatters of its face, like the flag of a ruined army.

"Daddy, come on." Sean turned to see his daughter crawling up the stairs. She reached the top and crawled through the doorway, pulling her legs in after her. In the light, he could see the tears on her face, the twist of anguish. "Daddy, please. Come on. Come on."

Sean put his hand on Katie's back. "Don't you remember me? I'm your husband. Don't you remember?"

She continued to work, slowly, her arms like shovels powered by a fading battery.

He lifted her from her place in the earth, dirt sifting from her body like a snowfall, and clutched her tightly to his chest. He rested his head against the blood-greased curve of her skull, cradled her forehead in his hand. "Stay with me."

Heather, one more time, from somewhere above him: "Daddy, oh no, please come up. Please."

"Get down here," Sean said. "Goddamn you, get down here."

The door shut, cutting off the wedge of light. He held his wife in his arms, rocking her back and forth, cooing into the ear that still remained.

He pulled her away, but she barely knew it. Everything was quiet now. Silence blew from the hole she had dug like smoke. She could feel what lay just beyond. The new countryside. The unspeaking multitude. Steeples and arches of bone; temples of silence. She felt the great shapes that moved there, majestic and unfurled, utterly silent, utterly dark.

He held her, breathing air onto the last cinder in her skull.

Her fingers scraped at empty air, the remains of her body engaged in this one final enterprise, working with a machine's unguided industry, divorced at last from its practical function. Working only because that was its purpose; its rote, inelegant chore.

# Acknowledgments

If a heart is a country, then here is an atlas to mine. These people are my cities, my rivers, my haunted forests. I owe them everything.

My friend and colleague Dale Bailey has been there since the beginning of this journey, offering good advice and stalwart friendship no matter the weather. My friendship with him has been one of the signal relationships of my life, and he has my faith and my loyalty until the end. Likewise Jeff and Ann VanderMeer: they've been my friends for over twenty years now; knowing them has made me a better writer and, more importantly, a better reader. They continue to enrich my life.

I'm grateful to April White, my dear friend and the first reader for many of these stories, for more than I have room to say in a stray sentence like this (it would take a library); to Neal Stanifer, for talking literature and laser guns with me over those many nights at The Avenue Pub in New Orleans; and to Chris Shanik, for realigning my perspective more than once.

Thanks to Lucius Shepard, whose influence on me has been profound, and whose subsequent friendship was a welcome surprise. (If my 21-year-old self had known that this would happen, he . . . well, never mind.)

Thanks to the people from my New Orleans life: Monte and Maura White, Jim McCallum, Ed and Mimi Sammarco, Jon and Vanessa Brink, Brian Jones (from whom I stole the title to "S.S."), Sara Danek, Ginger Lux, Anna Bourn, Sobha Ketterer, Kimy Brown, Vicki Robinson, Molly Knapp, John MacNichol, Wombat, Violet Vosper,

Rick and Trevor; and those who are gone: Craig Stevens, Duane Watts, and dear old Sunbeam. My years in New Orleans were among the happiest in my life, due in large part to these folks.

Thanks to the editors who bought these stories: Ellen Datlow (many times over!), Andy Cox, Terri Windling, Gary McMahon, and, of course, Kelly Link and Gavin J. Grant.

And thanks to the many, many others who offered friendship, wisdom, or a kick in the ass along the way: Pam Noles, Karen Tucker, Laird Barron, John Langan, Jeffrey Ford, Jeremy and Alexa Duncan, Katherine Min, Maureen McHugh, Mark Hartman, Paul Witcover, Theodora Goss, Andy Fox, Livia Llewellyn, Steve Berman, Veronica Schanoes, Glen Hirshberg, Michael Bishop, Jason Van Hollander, and everyone from the Sycamore Hill Writers Workshop, where I sometimes disappear for a week and pretend that the world is full of people who love stories.

# Publication History

# About the Author

Nathan Ballingrud (nathanballingrud.com) was born in Massachusetts in 1970 but has spent most of his life in the South. He's worked as a bartender in New Orleans and a cook on offshore oil rigs. His stories have appeared in several Year's Best anthologies, and he has twice won the Shirley Jackson Award. His second collection, *Wounds: Six Stories from the Border of Hell* includes the novella "The Visible Filth" which was filmed by Babak Anvari as *Wounds*. He lives in Asheville, North Carolina, with his daughter.

YOU HAVE
NEVER BEEN
HERE

*New and Selected Stories*

Mary
Rickert

Winner of the Shirley Jackson Award

"A few years ago Mary Rickert achieved the rare distinction of winning two World Fantasy Awards in one year. . . . The strangeness of Rickert's fiction is more than balanced by her acute insights into families and disturbed minds." — Gary K. Wolfe, *Chicago Tribune*

"Imbued with mythology, beasts, and fantastical transformations, Rickert captures the fanciful quality of regret and longing. . . . Rickert's blend of dark and whimsy is reminiscent of Angela Carter." — *Booklist*

paper · $16 · 9781618731104 | ebook · 9781618731111